The Liar's Tale
and Other Fibs

Lannah Battley

Fearneleaf Books

Published by Fearneleaf Books
fearneleaf@btinternet.com

Copyright © 2016 Lannah Battley
All rights reserved.

ISBN 978-0-9932236-2-4

Cover design by JD Smith Designs

These stories are works of fiction and, except in the case of historical fact, any resemblance to actual persons, living or dead, is purely coincidental.

Also by Lannah Battley

Either End of the Tunnel

Acknowledgements

My thanks to all the following for their help,
encouragement and expertise:

Angela Thomas, Geoff Willmetts,
Hope Mathews, Ingrid Fearne, J D Smith, Jen Green,
Lesley Milner, Nicola Radley, Paul Beardsley,
Ryan Fearne and Sarah LeFanu.

The
Liar's Tale
and other fibs

Introduction

Most of these stories were written a long time ago. At least one, has been overtaken by the advances of science but, mostly, editing has been minimal and it remains of its time. Here are some of the publishing details:

The Liar's Tale was published online at the SF Crowsnest website in 1999 and has remained available in their archive since 2001. However, at the request of the editor, the story within the story stood alone in *Noesis Science Fiction Magazine* #2, March 1999, under the title "Castaway".

Flagrance appeared in the Autumn 1995 issue of the science fiction and fantasy magazine, S*ubstance.*

Cyclops was published in *Despatches from the Frontiers of the Female Mind,* The Women's Press, 1985, editors Jen Green and Sarah Lefanu.

Information from a Philharmonic Spy, its original title, was published in the Winter 1994 issue of the science fiction and fantasy magazine S*ubstance* under the title *Communications from a Philharmonic Spy.*

Fear of the Alien reached the shortlist of five for the James White Award in 2002 but this is its first time in print.

The other stories are also unpublished until now. A couple of them are part of work in progress on planned novels.

LB

Contents

The Liar's Tale	1
Flagrance	25
Armies Of Martyrs	43
Darling Starlings	69
Cyclops	94
Meeting The Quota	116
Frankenstein On The Moon	140
Fear Of The Alien	166
Threll	181
Information From A Philharmonic Spy	203

THE LIAR'S TALE

Lorenz observed the woman through the spy-hole.

Bright reflections from the hygienic surfaces made him squint and feel glad that he had no need to live inside a steel box. Underfoot, shiny tinplate sloped to the central drainage grille and a gleaming gun-metal shelf bolted to one wall served as a bed. Nothing was movable apart from the prisoner. She sat still, however, with her elbows resting on the table, fingers woven through short tufty hair, the picture of despair.

As the sliding door clanged shut behind him, Lorenz perched opposite her on the smooth comfortless seat which, like the metallic table, was bolted to the floor.

He talked gently. "I don't believe you understand the seriousness of the charge, Kara."

"I do."

He talked tough. "You could die! The penalty for lying on this planet is death."

"Yes. I was brought up on Luthera."

"What can have possessed your sister to report you to the authorities?"

"Many things. Jealousy, resentment, loss of face."

"Why did Aurora feel like that?"

"It's too complicated to explain."

"Kara, we need to know! And why did she nominate the piece called 'Castaway' for special investigation?"

"Because I told her it was just a story."

Lorenz groaned. Somebody craved his scalp. His career had spiralled upward, the brilliant young advocate acquiring nothing but prestigious prosecutions until appointed to the defence of this impossibly hopeless case. The lawyer began to realise why defending counsel were so few on Luthera. Sooner or later their positions became untenable.

Now he experienced the feelings of every accused, the certainty of conviction and condemnation. What sort of defence existed? Only the one his enemies wanted.

Lorenz sighed. "To defend you, I shall have to commit a similar offence myself. They'll concentrate on 'Castaway'. What's on your record and what isn't will be important. You never actually had any military experience?"

"None. All my space experience was commercial with Interplanetary Freight."

"Then we'll have to fabricate some. If we can convince the court that your story is fact, a biographical account, then there's a good chance of clearing your name. I'll see what I can sort out about your employment record and a variety of other things then come back this evening to make more plans."

His smooth, dark hair came close to her tousled blonde-grey as he pressed her hand.

Thumping on the entry, Lorenz waited for the warder to look through the spy-hole then sidled across the narrow gap briefly offered. His heeltaps echoed along rule-straight corridors to the Central Record Unit.

Later, at home, he settled into a yielding armchair with a strong drink and began to reread 'Castaway'.

Remove legs at the first joint. Slit skin along the belly and detach from flesh before working away from the hind legs. Pull towards head and forelimbs, easing clear of the carcase.

Easy, huh? I had little loopy snares all over my side of the island but the fear of Ingram arriving to dish out retribution cramped my style as the mighty hunter.

But woman must eat. With emergency rations, water flowing abundantly and a vast choice of vegetation I'd survived. After three days, a tiny rabbit appeared in one of my traps, making me whoop for joy. I cooked it on the slim, cylindrical Heat-Facility from my suit's inner pockets.

Press Section A to release stand. Place on flat area or clamp for stability. Slide B to fan out upper container. Push C to heat. Use D to adjust temp.

Neat diagram and a lot easier than skinning a rabbit.

Despite my ineptitude, the meat tasted wonderful and as I sat overlooking the beach with the sun setting and breakers crashing, life seemed a little better. My jubilation had allowed me to forget the commander for a while but I knew not to be complacent. The bastard would catch up with me sooner or later.

INGRAM: *Supreme Commander Ingram Ingram brought to a successful close the long siege of the planet Romulus, acquiring for Ithaca and the Ithacan system much needed fertile territory. Tragically, after ten years campaigning, the Galaxy Hero's flagship, the Steeliteheart, was lost during the return journey. It is believed that the vessel's motion system failed. There are indications that Commander Ingram and his crew coasted on auxiliary to Remus (q.v), the nearest planet likely to sustain life.*

[See also Terraplanet Wars.]

Something like that. Some female crew called him Handy Andy. If you rejected his advances he made you out a useless officer. Welcoming overtures, however, meant advancement. Despite such peccadilloes, many admired him as a capable commander and strategist.

Remus had breathable atmosphere and looked attractive from orbit with mountains, lakes and vegetation. Half the crew, me included, descended in scout cars to establish camp and find much needed food resources. We made for the larger of two major continents, a huge land mass which looked like a Catherine wheel throwing out great spatterings of islands into the vast green oceans.

"Why's this place never been colonised?" muttered the suspicious-minded.

We soon discovered. Having almost made landfall, a devastating tempest plucked us up and tossed and buffeted the scout way off course.

Scout cars are built to survive on almost any surface. Plunging into the dark Remusian sea was frightening but we soon resurfaced and maintained a crackly vocal contact with the mothership. Though unable to lift off while the storm blew, the worst we expected to suffer was sea-sickness and a few bruises from loosened gear skidding up and down the deckings.

Instead, we landed upon a jagged rock. The scout broke up, despite the enormous tensile strength of its outer skin. The sound of the Abandon Ship came as a shock. I'd never heard one for real in all my years as a fighting woman.

Bobbing to the surface from an escape tube, my inflatable blossomed with a sharp tug of the ripcord just as in a lifetime of drills. Unlike practices in space, the craft bucked like a demented see-saw. After hauling myself in by the attach-line, I strapped up and surveyed the mountainous seas from a crest.

Far ahead, other flates, tiny specks, corkscrewed. Meanwhile, to stern a vast black wall of water swept towards me. When I'd ridden it out and lifted up the further side of the following trough, the others had disappeared.

Plunging once more, a helmet appeared in the sea, slithering at speed along the side of the flatable, face down, body beneath. Desperately I unzipped the port, stretched out and grasped a waterlogged shoulder-strap. Hauling amid cascades of ocean, the deadweight tumbled through the strap. Managing to turn the bulky form over my heart sank. It was Ingram. A horrible shock. The last person I'd wish to save. He was coming round and I didn't feel ruthless enough to tip him back in the ocean.

Continually pounded, we were driven at last in lowering darkness upon a shelving coast which, by daylight, proved to be a picture-idyll of long, tree lined, sandy beaches. Unfortunately, horrendous screechings echoed from inland. I walked miles along the shore in both directions looking for a way around the trees. Meanwhile, Ingram attempted to contact the other scout cars and the mothership.

The flate contained a lot of survival equipment and converted according to Instruction Code Z94 into a dwelling but I elected to sleep in full spacesuit outside.

"What's the matter, Lieutenant? Don't you trust me? If we're going by the book, then I'll swing seniority and order you to penetrate the tree cover in the morning to find water inland. Water tablets won't last forever and, let's face it, you're not making a very good job of finding any other way round. Draw your sidearm when you reach the trees."

At dawn, helmet hooked at the waist, I stepped from daylight into green luminosity and began pressing blue markers into alien tree trunks. Why I needed to brave the forest alone was perfectly clear to me. Ingram knew I'd never submit to his advances. He'd tried plenty of times in the past. This was my punishment. On top of still being a lieutenant. Also, though he might be a great strategist, I suspected that when it came to real action, he might be a coward. Hearing the wild animal noises had probably decided him on not chancing his arm in the interior.

He needn't have worried. My path emerged at last into a stony clearing. A large bird with trailing tail feathers fled into the underbrush. Another suddenly appeared and let out the horrifying shriek which had kept us out of the woodland. The first creature returned and the second swung its long tattered tail into the air and splayed it open like a giant fan of playing cards. What had been dull and dusty was revealed as an iridescently purple ten of spades. The two birds went off screeching into the trees.

At evening, I emerged onto a high plateau. A panoramic view revealed the geography of an island. Dense treetops spread in all directions, affording the occasional glimpse of surf-fringed beaches and, beyond, an endless expanse of dark green sea.

Without a flate, I slept in my suit with helmet half adjusted and woke to the sound of water. The stream cascaded down the further side of the hill and led me in the course of the day to the sea and a smooth beach where gentle night-time waves lulled me to sleep. The next night, on my return journey, I slept on the plateau again and filled two waterskins from the stream the following morning.

Despite efforts every evening, the communications Stud on my collar failed to pick up Ingram or anybody else. Desperately hoping for other survivors, I left the Comstud in Receive.

Back on the beach, the commander was still alone pacing back and forth, a zip-rifle hanging loosely from his hand. As soon as I approached and spoke to him, worried as to what might have happened, he turned, pointed the gun at me and snarled, "You're under arrest, Lieutenant."

"Arrest! Why?"

"Desertion."

"How can that be? I explored inland on your orders."

"But you've been away three nights. A very dangerous thing with the two of us split up and surrounded by potentially lethal animals."

I threw down the skins hauled from the spring. "The water was a long way, Commander, and heavy."

Insubordination. Arguing with a senior officer... (Section B37).

Incensed by his attitude, I failed to tell him about the peacocks or that we were on an island.

DISCIPLINARY CODE Section B55: To withhold significant information from an officer in circumstances necessitating full facts, constitutes Dereliction of Duty...

"You're confined to barracks, Lieutenant. Relinquish all weapons."

I threw my handgun on the sand.

"Fighting knife?"

"Lost at sea."

"Typical."

That was rich! He arrived on the island only thanks to me and with no survival gear of his own.

"Zip-rifle?"

"You hold it, Commander. It's from my flate. And the knife at your belt."

"Get inside the flate. Remove your spacesuit and place it by the entrance. I shall then come and interview you."

Ah-oh. This sounded like a Handy Andy technique: confined to barracks, give up your weapons, take off your clothes.

A hasty search of the flate's interior pouches produced emergency food capsules and snares which fitted neatly into the inner pockets of my suit. Quickly disrobing, I snapped helmet and suit into a carry-loop. A utility knife, found among cooking equipment, slid neatly out of sight under a squab as Ingram entered.

DISCIPLINARY CODE Section P74: The penalty for assaulting a colleague is imprisonment in a Military Jail for a period of one year. Subsequent offences incur higher penalties and the risk of expulsion from the Space Service.

"You could make life so much easier for yourself, Lieutenant. If we shared this flate as sexual partners, to our mutual satisfaction, then the military charge could be dropped."

"I'm a soldier, Commander, not a prostitute."

"You've always been the one for me, you know. So we could be alone, I never even attempted to contact the ship or the others lost overboard."

"Then you're a damn fool. (*B47: Verbally Abusing a Superior*) There must be something in the manual forbidding an officer from neglecting his crew for the sake of personal pleasure."

"Careful, Lieutenant!" he whispered. "Duty and discipline dictate that you accept the way of living prescribed by your superior officer."

Suddenly Ingram sprang, making me stumble as his far heavier body weight landed on me.

"What does the book say about raping junior officers?" I screamed.

"You're asking for it, Lieutenant. Your tongue's hanging out for it."

Though a high-ranking officer, there was nothing rusty about his combat technique. Grappling on the floor, employing every dirty trick known to fighting woman, his bulk sapped my strength. Suddenly Ingram lifted himself to rip at my undersuit. Seeing the opening, I rolled, kicked and threw.

His knife clicked open as he bounced back off the flate wall, his reactions far faster than anticipated. Scrabbling too late for my own pitiful knife, his full weight flopped upon me again. To risk a serious wounding seemed madness with no professional medical care at hand.

My only option was submission. My state of mind alternated between hatred and self-disgust. When Ingram squirmed off me, wild fury took over. That and my hidden knife gave me the slight advantage of surprise. I slashed him halfway up his forearm, making him howl with pain and rage, then shoved him over while he was off-balance. I grabbed my suit bundle and fled up the beach and into the trees.

DISCIPLINARY CODE Section P75: The penalty for assaulting a superior officer is imprisonment for five years in a Military Jail, followed by Expulsion with Ignominy from the Space Service. A longer incarceration may be imposed at the discretion of the Court Martial President.

No mention of provocation. Anyway, what chance the word of a lieutenant against a Galaxy Hero?

I removed my blue marker trail as it led me all the way back to the stream and, reaching there by dusk, deemed it safe to halt and washed away Ingram's dregs.

My new, solitary life on the other side of the island had its constraints. A permanent fire for cooking would also have been an excellent signal to would-be rescuers but Ingram might detect the smoke. My only signal was a huge SOS mapped out on My Beach with a snapped off branch and heaped over with rocks, seaweed, anything which could attract an overflying craft.

Cooking with the little Heat Facility produced no smoke or flame but I fretted that the aroma would betray my whereabouts.

Instruction Z48: For the sake of hygiene and tidiness, burn or bury bones and entrails not used for stock. Food scraps could attract unwelcome carrion-seeking animals.

Ingram had the only spade.

One evening, a sudden sensation of being watched made me grab the knife, my only weapon and always within reach, and roll behind a boulder. There was no zip of a rifle-shot. In the golden glow of the setting sun, two eyes gleamed. My heart beat fast as a feline slid past my bivouac to the rubbish dump, depository of putrefying rabbit innards.

Tawny-furred and not quite big enough to be a threat,

the cat had pointed ears sprouting long tufts of hair. The creature, a lynx perhaps, gnawed blissfully, eyes closed, head to one side.

"Here, Puddy, Puddy, Puddy," I whispered.

The cat gave me an irritated glance and slunk off into the trees.

Instruction Z39: Be prepared in difficult survival conditions to consider all manner of plants and animals, which initially might seem abhorrent, as potential food.

Never once did I consider the cat for the pot although she began to visit my camp regularly. Instead, she enjoyed lights and other scraps during food preparation and the occasional cooked titbit thrown at her feet. Her femininity was simply a presumption based on the dainty way she washed her blood-stained paws after gorging on rabbit entrails.

Her name metamorphosed from Puddy to Purdy.

The wind tore my bracken bivouac to shreds one night. By morning a full gale made me clasp the bole of a tree, the only effective method to avoid being swept away. The storm blew stronger and howled louder inside the wood, perhaps due to a wind tunnel effect. Yet many of the tree trunks were several metres in diameter so the forest had survived the planet's weather over countless years.

Purdy pranced by, tail high, and leapt up a tree. Deciding to follow her example, I found the smooth bark presented difficulties for me.

The blue markers now came into their own. Some were already incorporated in my SOS. One by one, I extracted the rest from my outer pockets and used them like pitons to climb upwards.

Fighting through masses of ribbon-like foliage which swayed with my every movement, I emerged into a different world, a moving green cathedral whose lofty vaulting whispered constantly. Plantain fonts, leafy balconies, bosky walkways and living floorboards quivered in a stiff breeze.

Tentatively standing upright, I balanced along a wide moss-covered branch to an arboreal pulpit and wedged myself in the upper section until the nave stopped moving and verdant light dimmed to blackness, bringing sleep.

In the vestry, Ingram jumped out on me from a pile of hassocks. I fell to the floor screaming and wrestling but nothing would shift him. His hands mauled and kneaded me. Though my head twisted rapidly from side to side his viscid, probing tongue found mouth, ears, eyes. Suddenly aware of a knife in my hand, I ripped his body from crotch to heart. His saturating blood began to drown me in a crimson sea. Wallowing helplessly beside the hulk of the scout car on a silty red seabed, a jagged edge of the wreck ground my face in time with the swell.

I awoke to find Purdy giving me a loving but painfully abrasive wash.

The pulpit became home. Up there, Ingram was less likely to stumble across me, particularly after I'd found easier routes into the canopy and removed the tell-tale markers.

A hot calm followed. The storm had honed my SOS almost smooth. Each day at dawn I'd check my traps then labour on the beach with the Heat-Facility and the Com-stud lapping up the sun. By midday, fierce heat drove me to the cool greenness of the pulpit where I fashioned new snares to replace those swept away by the storm. There were always spares in my pockets.

Instruction Z21: Retain as much equipment for survival as possible about your person in case a precipitous retreat becomes necessary. Spacesuit pockets and pouches, both internal and external, are there to be used.

Constantly moving through the canopy, I learnt to

leap from branch to branch with great fluency. Though a novice compared to Purdy, she seemed to delight in my new-found skill. We played stalking games through the leaf cover until she grew bored and stretched along a bough, one paw dangling nonchalantly.

With the SOS restored, there was more time to consider priorities.

Z Instructions recommended stranded personnel leave their Comstud in Transmit, an open invitation to Ingram in my circumstances. Mine remained in the pulpit set to Receive, the theory being that, up there, if any signal sounded with Ingram in the vicinity, he would have difficulty locating the direction.

Of course, a fire should be burning as a beacon in a prominent position, belching thick smoke into the sky by day and burning bright at night. Ingram made such a thing impossible. The more I thought about it the more intolerable it seemed. The only solution was to return to Ingram's Beach. If other survivors had turned up there I'd feel reasonably safe and might be bold enough to denounce him. Otherwise, I'd have to work out how to kill him even though he had a zip-rifle and a fighting knife. My one advantage was the ability to move rapidly through the canopy like a cat, unheard and unseen.

New mobility enabled me to explore the beaches on my side of the island, using blue markers up in the leaf cover with equanimity. Discovering no other survivors, I decided to return to Ingram's Beach and find out how he had fared in the hurricane before checking the beaches on that coast. I'd remain unobserved, unless he were in the direst straits.

In sweltering weather, wearing only an undersuit, I moved through the canopy towards the island's central plateau, spiking in markers from my helmet hitched at the waist and keeping the watercourse within earshot. Only ten minutes had passed when I heard the unmistakable zizz of a zip-rifle.

Easing myself onto a branch with a view of the stream, a marker dropped to the ground. About to descend, the commander suddenly materialised below and I drew back into the foliage.

He wore a filthy undersuit. Ragged bandages swathed his arm and ammunition belts criss-crossed his sweat-stained chest. Mad-eyed, lean, with stubbly beard and hollow cheeks, he clung to the zip-rifle as if it were a life-raft.

Seeing the blue disc, Ingram sprang forward with an exclamation of satisfaction then called, "Lieutenant! Come out! I won't harm you. No hard feelings!" But his rifle was held at the ready and his eyes gleamed vindictively. After pacing round like a caged animal he leapt at the marker and kicked it in fury.

"Damn you, Lieutenant! I'll find you and have my fill of you. Then you'll suffer! Every indignity. Before you die. Before I eat you. When they come to rescue me I'll say 'Lieutenant? What lieutenant?'" And he cackled crazily.

Silently retreating, my helmet caught on a branch. Markers clattered and bounced against branches and tree trunk to land at Ingram's feet.

The commander let out a bellow of triumph.

Heart bumping, I swarmed up into the higher canopy.

Ingram struggled into my translucent, green world and began to follow the trail of markers. I had knife and helmet, nothing more.

Instruction Z21: Retain as much equipment for survival as possible about your person…

Silently cursing my clumsiness, I watched in despair from the cathedral's vaulted ceiling as he traversed the nave and climbed the pulpit. Ingram reached inside and lifted my spacesuit like a trophy but let go as a snarling creature rose up.

The commander backed away as Purdy arched her back, displaying a jaggedly erect tail and bared fangs. His rifle fell to the transept floor and bounced before rattling through a crevice into the notional crypt.

Looking around in panic, he jumped to the aisle and scrabbled around for a way down while Purdy stood with fur on end, spitting hate. Before long Ingram stumbled through a gap joining his weapon below.

"I'll be back, you bitch!" he howled.

More than likely the commander would return in his space suit, armour enough against a tiger, and attempt to shoot Purdy for the pot. I rearranged the markers to lead from the stream to somewhere totally irrelevant then moved from the pulpit, with some sadness, to a small niche with the advantage of overlooking My Beach.

As we sat over our evening rabbit, I pondered how long it might be before Ingram returned. The trip to His Beach and back could take four days. On the other hand, if he had moved camp to the plateau, where there was water and a cooking fire would provide a good marker signal for would-be rescuers.

A climb to the roof of the forest next day would confirm whether smoke rose from the plateau, warning enough of the commander's rapid return. Perhaps I'd work out a way to tempt Ingram by way of the markers into a lethal trap.

That night the wind blew strong and, claws and fingers splayed, Purdy and I clung on as the canopy bucked and swayed.

A calming dawn brought fitful sleep until a great pinging sound began to reverberate through the canopy.

Purdy leapt from the niche and fled.

As the bleep kept repeating, monotonous, loud, insistent, shock subsided into comprehension. The Comstud was at last picking up a signal.

I gazed at it, mesmerized. Could the commander be

tempting me to reveal my whereabouts? Was he listening close by for the giveaway signal, waiting to pounce?

As my hand hovered over the off button, the tone died and a casual voice began to speak: "This is Rescue Ship Hermes at thirty-six macros, homing in and observing the surface of Remus. We're searching for survivors of the battleship Steeliteheart. If you hear us, please switch to Send and make yourselves known."

I kept quiet, waiting and listening. There was no reply from Ingram.

"This is Rescue Ship Hermes at thirty-four macros, homing in and observing the surface..."

Ingram could never produce this relaxed voice.

Thirty-three macros, thirty-two.

Purdy returned cautiously and sniffed at the bed.

Thirty-one. I would have to make my presence known soon and so would Ingram. If he was on the plateau, the ship might see him.

Thirty macros. I must be rescued first!

Transmission of a brief greeting, name and rank, brought an immediate response.

"Your communication received! How many are you? We have very limited space in the first instance."

"There are two of us. Me and the commander."

"We're monitoring weather conditions as we descend. Touchdown and lift-off must be very swift. As you know, this is a dangerous planet for landings."

"Agreed."

"Your signal's clear, Lieutenant, and we're receiving a homing bleep from your Comstud. Muster immediately at a suitable landing place. No luggage. Communicators must be on your persons and in Receive."

Half expecting Ingram to leap out, I scuttled down the beach and stood beside the windswept SOS feeling exposed.

On an impulse I unclipped the communicator, threw it onto the sand and rushed back to the niche. Purdy, recovered from the alien noise, was curled on the bed. Sweeping her up, I'd slid her inside my half zipped spacesuit before she realised what was happening and, humming all the while, slithered to the ground. She struggled a little but began to purr as we waltzed down the beach to a hoarsely crooned dance tune.

A small, silent craft landed neatly in the middle of the 'O' of the SOS.

Purdy squirmed and dug in her claws but I gritted my teeth and kept her clasped firmly to my breast. As we approached the rescue ship, a port slid open and a head appeared. Darting eyes took in my status flashes.

"Make it snappy, Lieutenant," called my rescuer. "Get the commander here soonest. We've got to lift off within minutes."

"This is the commander." I nodded at the cat in my arms. "Commander Purdy, my constant companion."

"A full-blown commander, eh?" he laughed. "Get strapped in fast. And that animal too. I didn't see it, okay?"

The craft rose. I looked down on the receding island. No smoke was visible on the plateau.

DISCIPLINARY CODE Section B55: To withhold significant information from an officer in circumstances necessitating full facts, constitutes Dereliction of Duty. Penalties range from one month's imprisonment in a Military Jail to the death sentence where the lives of other personnel are jeopardised.

Commander Purdy and I have lived happily ever after. My property on Ithaca has in its grounds a large and complicated jungle-gym incorporating much foliage and covered by translucent green synthetic. We often disport ourselves there. Our neighbours are tolerant. They expect the sole survivor of the Steeliteheart to be slightly crackpot.

"Lies! All lies!" shouted the Prosecutor. "We can trace no planets bearing the names in the document or any military vessel called the Steeliteheart."

"Hardly surprising," replied Lorenz. "The universe is much bigger than the Prosecutor comprehends. The Ithacan system is beyond the reach of Luthera's space technology. Perhaps I should apply for an adjournment to bring in the necessary experts."

"Certainly not. I'm content to proceed. We have other inconsistencies to follow up. We cannot trace this particular species of lynx, for instance."

"The animal, called a caracal, still exists on Earth. The Romans once used the cats for hunting in desert areas."

Lorenz had chosen the now unfamiliar name from an obscure reference work to "identify" Purdy, thinking it might wrong foot the prosecution. Therefore he felt very gratified when the Prosecutor sent minions scurrying to also scour texts before calling Aurora.

"My sister started writing when she returned to Luthera after retiring from Interplanetary Freight. 'Castaway' particularly impressed me and I mentioned it to a friend as an exciting, if difficult, period in my sister's life."

"With what result?"

"He spoke to Kara about her adventures marooned on Remus. My sister said none of it happened. My friend, rather peeved, told me. I was mortified. When I spoke to Kara she laughed and said it was just a story."

"A story?" interrupted the Arbiter. "Like a press report?"

"No," said Aurora. "Just lies."

There was a hush in the court and Aurora looked around in sudden alarm.

Lorenz jumped up. "Are you sure that you're not lying? Your sister returned to share the family home which had been solely yours till then. Her accounts of life in space and faraway places made her popular with your friends. Didn't her social success make you resentful and provoke you into getting her into trouble?"

"Why, no!" said Aurora, genuinely shocked.

Lorenz sat down, aware that her sincerity had gone against him.

The usher called Kara.

"Caracals exist on Earth," said the Prosecutor. "Have you ever been there?"

"We had to put down there for repairs once."

"For how long?"

"Seven years."

"For repairs?"

"There was a war waging. We couldn't get off again."

"What did you do all that time?"

"General maintenance duties and, in our spare time, watching video. But eventually boredom set in so I studied quite a lot: Earthian languages, old texts, stuff like that."

"What other evidence is required?" the Prosecutor asked the court. "Earthians are notorious liars and they enmeshed this poor Lutheran in their ways."

"Not proven and irrelevant," shouted Lorenz.

"Then there is your personal record," purred the Prosecutor. "It shows that you served with Interplanetary Freight throughout your working life, never as a combatant."

"After two years on Earth, I volunteered for the Neovegan Military Service, the only way to get off planet. Though against company rules, a colleague and an Earthian friend covered for me."

"Neovegas is not Romulus or the equally mythical Remus."

"After training, I was seconded to the Ithacan Space Force and felt thrilled to travel at last into deep space. Passing an endurance and survival test won me a posting to Romulus. The siege ended two years later."

"According to the document 'Castaway', you spent the rest of your days on Ithaca with this creature."

"Clearly, not the rest of my days. I had to return to Earth for the sake of my friends. Leaving Purdy on Ithaca was a wrench but she has a good home."

Kara thought that Lorenz's version of her story, transforming it into reality, was working well so far but felt intensely worried that she might forget some of the important aspects of its complexities. However, when asked to explain some of the detail of 'Castaway', she did so, giving the Prosecutor a contemptuous look for his ignorance.

"Hundreds of creatures were transported to Remus when it was used as an animal reserve. The scheme didn't last long because landing and lift-off were so hazardous. Many craft crash-landed. Rabbits, peacocks and the single caracal probably reached the island from a wrecked transporter like me."

Kara tried to relax but stress seemed to be knotting her neck and shoulder muscles and she felt ready to scream.

"These things should be made clear," snapped the Prosecutor. "True writing should give the relevant facts. The quotations from instruction manuals in your account are excellently factual but as for the rest… The writer's reaction to her commander's importunate advances, for example, is very suspect."

"Advances! You know how women react, do you? I thought you dealt only in truth. How can you project yourself into another person's feelings on facts alone? To predict how someone might behave in a given situation calls for imagination. A kind of fiction!"

"Fiction! Is that what this piece of writing is?"

Kara felt her patience and self-control snap. "Yes, yes, yes! Fiction! What's wrong with that? The ossified laws of Luthera are crazy!"

When the hubbub died down the Prosecutor said, "Fiction, any fiction, is the first step to corruption and leads to the destruction of integrity."

"There's no integrity here. People lie to convince others they're telling the truth. The whole system's truth is built on lies."

Court ushers beat their gavels till the sudden uproar subsided.

"I urge immediate sentencing," shouted the Prosecutor into the silence.

The Arbiter shook his head. "The defendant has clearly changed her plea to guilty. An adjournment seems in order until tomorrow morning."

"Pity you got mad," muttered Lorenz later. "I must be crazy to continue with your case but I'll do it. Aurora's rather attractive, isn't she?"

"What's that got to do with anything?"

"Your sister deeply regrets the position she's put you in."

"How thoughtful!"

"She had no idea that the death penalty was still invoked for lying. After the adjournment, she'll refuse to appear for the prosecution. With the way the law stands, we can't say Aurora lied, so we'll suggest she misunderstood what you said."

"And turn herself into a true liar."

"Unfortunately, the state will continue with the prosecution. When the court reconvenes you must again maintain that 'Castaway' and all your writings are true. I shall plead insanity on your behalf."

"Insanity!"

"Yes. The death penalty will be avoided and I'll be able to work on getting you an Exile Order. It'll be a long hard slog and you may not get to see me again in private. That's why I want you to accept any rare opportunities for visitors."

"There's nobody who'd visit."

"Yes. Aurora."

"Aurora!"

"Please see her. It's important."

The case took the course which Lorenz predicted.

A mental patient's accommodation proved to be identical to a criminal's. In her sterile, shiny cell, deprived of books, writing materials, anything which might relieve boredom, Kara's life was a limbo of elongated time.

She endured this eternity of glossy nothingness, clinging to sanity by creating further fictions within her head until Aurora stepped diffidently over the metallic threshold. Blinking in the harsh metallic glare, her sister sat down and stared mournfully across the glittering table.

"Lorenz has gone."

"Where?"

"Neovegas. He was about to be prosecuted for lying."

"Hah!"

"On your behalf. He's been whipping up support for your Exile Order among writers on other planets but our administration hold all those people in contempt. It's made his position very difficult."

"You seem to know a lot about his position."

"I got to know him – quite well."

"And now he's run out on both of us."

"No! Lorenz said he was going to spin a web of lies of interplanetary proportions. It frightens me, Kara. Now he's asked me to smuggle this message."

"Message?"

"The Neovegan Ambassador's been requesting your

extradition on behalf of Ithacan justice system over a long period. The Government's been saying you're of unsound mind, therefore can't face the rigours of a trial elsewhere."

"So much for Lorenz's ploy."

"But now Lorenz has arranged for a representative from Ithaca to attend a court hearing in person."

"How very interesting," said Kara, knowing that Ithaca only existed in her own imagination.

"And there's an excellent chance you'll be handed over to him. Lorenz said that providing you plead guilty to all accusations, there's a strong possibility that the Supreme Arbiter will grant extradition."

"They'll never let me go."

"Lorenz is determined to get you off planet, Kara, and when he does, I'm going to join him."

"Join him now. Otherwise you might wait forever."

"No! When this diplomat comes, they'll relent and you'll be taken to Ithaca."

"Don't bank on it," said Kara, smiling bleakly at her sister's gullibility.

Time stretched, an inexorable void in her glistening box. Kara began to think she would see nothing but its hard sheen ever again until, one morning, she was hustled to the High Court.

The Supreme Arbiter, dressed in full regalia, sat flanked by officials. Before him stood a middle-aged, dark-suited man and two youngish women wearing the black overgown of legal office.

"You are summoned to the High Court in the interests of universal truth and justice," intoned the Arbiter. "Ithaca, on behalf of all the Ithacan nations in the distant Meelai Galaxy, after making petition through the diplomats of various nearer planets and planetary federations, have now sent their own representative. The Ithacan Plenipotentiary will read the charges."

The dark-suited diplomat spoke slowly in a dense foreign accent. "Lieutenant Kara Oana, you are charged with dereliction of duty and that, by omission, you caused the death of a colleague. We now have proof positive that your superior officer died on the reservation planet Remus. His emaciated remains have recently been recovered and, as a result, we are again requesting an extradition order. I should tell you that our administration is determined that you shall return and stand trial for the murder of Galaxy Hero, Supreme Commander Ingram Ingram."

"This is not a trial but I must ask the prisoner how she would plead," said the Arbiter.

"Guilty," Kara whispered.

Sitting beside the Arbiter, her former Prosecutor stared grimly. Satisfaction gleamed in his eyes.

"Hearing adjourned."

Back in her cell, she paced. Her mind, deprived of any matter worth thinking about, suddenly whirled with apprehensions. If Lorenz could persuade so many people to lie on her behalf, then perhaps corruption was the inevitable outcome of fiction. She tossed and turned all night.

Next morning, the court proceedings were formal but brief. The designation 'unsound mind' was revoked and charges under Lutheran law set aside so that an immediate Exile Order could be issued. She was committed to the care of the Ithacan representative who nodded vindictively. Hurried through the building and into a closed van, Kara found herself sitting beside him.

The representative scowled but once the door shut he chuckled and, accent gone, whispered, "Listen. When we reach the spaceport look dejected, bowed down. Whatever you do, don't smile."

They emerged from the vehicle linked by handcuffs and, surrounded by his entourage, they walked to the launch pad. Kara dragged along, hunched, reluctant, staring at the ground.

At the foot of the hatchway, stood the Prosecutor. Kara's heart gave a lurch. The plot had been uncovered and all was lost!

They drew level. She saw him smile for the first and only time.

"The truth will out," he hissed as they began to climb.

FLAGRANCE

The rumour spread. Doc Sanderson lay dying. Family and friends gathered in the living room of his cottage while admirers and acquaintances spilt over the scant front garden into the village street beyond. The throng spread to the market place and, particularly crowded, the Red Dragon, also known as the *Ddraig Goch*.

Sadness was expressed at the imminent passing of a great man but many felt anticipation for the almighty wake which would follow. "The end of an era" was uttered over many a pint in both Welsh and English as well as the question, "How old was he, anyway?"

In the upstairs bedroom, Nerys, his granddaughter, held his hand. Her cousin, Owen, looked on.

"You don't remember Flagrance, do you?" he quavered. "Or Larking Brown Label? Not even television or advertising. We're all third world countries now. Less than third, fourth."

To her disgust, Nerys heard Owen snort and mutter, "Not the good old days again."

She blotted a burgeoning tear. Grandfather could ramble on as much as he liked but she would stay with him till the end.

"And you don't remember the Great British Crime Wave either, or the end of civilisation as we knew it."

"No, Grandpa."

"Of course you don't. It was over seventy years ago."

He gave a chesty sigh.

"I seem to have out-lived two whole generations."

"That's because you're such a clever doctor. People have come from miles around to be here."

"They know I'm dying, that's why."

"No!" said Nerys. "They're just concerned about your health. You're the most respected person in the community. It's your knowledge that's kept it going."

Sanderson began a laugh, which turned into a cough.

"What an old fraud I am," he whispered when Nerys had administered sips of water. "I was the cause of the end of civilisation as we…"

"No!"

"It," grunted Owen, who was staring disconsolately from the window at the crowd below.

"I was never a Doctor of Medicine."

"We know that, Grandpa. But you've been a wonderful healer with your potions. Aunt Bertha used to say you must have been a pharmacist."

"Did she now? Good guess but wrong. I was a chemist."

"Isn't that the same?"

"Not quite. I didn't work in a pharmacy. I had a degree in chemistry and a doctorate and, though I say so as shouldn't, was considered pretty brilliant. But the government cut all funding for research so I found myself the highest paid commercial position I could. In London with Contralto Perfumes."

"Perfumes?" said Owen, forgetting his determination to ignore his grandfather's ramblings.

"It seems strange now, I know, that money for vital research couldn't be found yet the producer of a useless luxury commodity would pay highest in the land for a first-rate chemist. But that's how things were before the end of civilisation."

"As we knew it," intoned Owen under his breath.

"Bernard O. Bass who built up Contralto was a real go-getter…"

His eyelids drooped and closed.

'Sanderson, we're a very successful company but we're going to be more than that. We're going to be great! The opposition will have no chance. Contralto is going to grab all the shekels in perfumery because you, Sanderson, are going to invent the ultimate perfume.'

Grandpa's eyes opened.

"You've seen all those crappy adverts on TV about the perfume that makes all the men swarm after a girl, haven't you?" he said. "Well, you're going to make me a scent that really does it. That was a tall order, even for me, but if anybody could do it… Money was no object. I had a modern laboratory in West London with hand-picked staff and could requisition any equipment I liked."

Owen moved closer to the bed, frowning. "He hasn't told me this one before."

"What I didn't have was time. Bass was an impatient man. However, in just over six months we produced a small amount of perfume which reached his specification and some trials were run."

"And did it work? Really work?"

"Oh yes. The perfume had – that effect on people. But it was extremely expensive to produce so had to be aimed at the absolutely upper echelon in the market, the stinking rich, you might say, with suitably opulent advertisements."

Sanderson closed his eyes.

In an idyllic country garden in soft focus, a stunning actress, not quite showing her nipples, leads a handsome, utterly smitten man through French windows into a manor house beyond the means of all but a millionaire. She trails shot silk up thickly carpeted stairs to her sumptuous boudoir rich with hangings. The compelling music, also hideously expensive, swells to mask the sharp intake of breath when the price is mentioned.

His eyes opened again.

"But it had cachet! It sold! All the same, Bass wasn't satisfied."

"What a horrible man!" said Nerys, incensed.

"Oh, he was pleased. He doubled my salary and I put a deposit on a house I'd set my heart on. He had every right to be happy. He was making pots of money out of Exclusif, which he insisted on calling it. A run-of-the-mill name, I thought. 'You might as well call it Expensif and be done with it,' I said. But Bass had made up his mind. He still wanted me to produce the same kind of perfume for the mass market so that he could have his 'This-Brings-The-Fellows-Flocking-For-Real' advert."

'Expensif – I mean Exclusif – is brilliant, my boy, but now we need something we can smother the market with. Then Contralto will be the market so far as perfumery is concerned. What we want you to do now is to somehow produce a cheap version of Exclusif.'

"It took a while but I did it – and I chose the name. That was Flagrance."

Nerys frowned. "And did that cause the end of civil…?"

"Not Flagrance Mark I. It was a great success and Bass had the TV advert he'd dreamed of. The pretty young girl drawing the men and the boys like bees to a honey pot, moths to the flame, iron filings to a magnet. The voice-over at the end said, 'Contralto's Flagrance: Irresistible.' And it was."

"So what went wrong?"

His account was punctuated with pauses and often his voice slurred. Now, a long silence yawned before he continued.

"Bernard Oliver Bass, Owen. Sales were booming, the graphs were shooting through the office ceilings. He was a millionaire ten times over and he'd saturated the market. But he hadn't eradicated the opposition completely. He summoned me to his plush Mayfair office. 'Sanderson,' he said, 'Flagrance is a winner but now it's got to finish off the competition once and for all. I want you to produce a stronger version.'"

'Stronger B.O.?'

'Yes. More of the ingredient that, that – er attracts, er – makes it irresistible.'

'I don't think I can do that. It would be dangerous.'

'Poppycock. You produce Flagrance Mark II and we'll have another major sales campaign with a wonderful new TV ad.'

"I was horrified but you couldn't argue with B.O. when he was like that. I kept repeating that it would be dangerous and he kept saying 'no, it wouldn't' and 'who cares?'"

"Dangerous, Grandpa?"

Sanderson seemed to be rallying with thoughts of the past.

"I'd produced a perfume that had a built-in attractor but it wasn't totally irresistible. It was as close to the edge as you could get. That was its beauty. To take it further would make it entirely compulsive. I started looking around to see if I could find some other job in pure research but there wasn't a hope. Nothing but recession, recession, cuts, cuts, cuts. So I had no choice. I went ahead. The new advert was brilliant but didn't say that the formula had changed. Only Bass and I knew that and a few senior staff at the factory. So far as everyone else was concerned it was just the pre-Christmas campaign to retain the bulk of the market. That Christmas! That was the last truly commercial, plastic overdraft, computerised cash-register Christmas. 'The ultimate perfume' was what the voice-over said at the end of the ad and it proved to be prophetic."

"What happened?"

"The sales drive was a huge success. The old stock of Flagrance was soon exhausted and the new formula began to hurtle across the counters. It was disaster from then on."

"But why, Grandpa?"

"Women like to attract men, the men they fancy anyway, but Flagrance II turned them into bitches on heat. Everybody was attracted regardless of the wearer's feelings. That was the beginning of the Great Crime Wave. Rape became a daily occurrence on a vast scale. I told Bass that the cause was Flagrance but he dismissed the information as nonsense. The police began to investigate Contralto after a tip-off from an anonymous phone-caller, who was me. Sales were falling, even before doubts were openly expressed. Women had stopped buying Flagrance – apart from nymphomaniacs and those who wanted to sue for rape. But suddenly men, well some men, were buying in bulk, especially in spray form. They roamed the cities at night looking for anybody they could vaguely desire as a victim. One puff and their lust became unstoppable. All kinds of perversions were being satiated. No man, woman or dog was safe. Gangs roamed the city streets and battered their way into chemists and department stores to ransack the stocks of Flagrance. There was a black market in the stuff which was run as viciously as the drugs market. In fact, for some, it was a drug."

Sanderson covered his face with leathery age-spotted hands.

"Flagrance II smelt wonderful but was a truly nasty substance. When the police questioned Bass he insisted that I had assured him that exhaustive tests had proved the safety of the product. It was my word against his. He was a multimillionaire so I got the blame. Within a day the sale of Flagrance was officially banned and all stocks called in. Bass sacked me."

"What a bastard. What happened to him?"

"I'm coming to that, Owen."

He struggled to a sitting position.

"I was developing an antidote and took all my work home to the basement of my house together with as much equipment as possible and set up my own laboratory. I tried to get funding for the research but my picture kept appearing in the papers and on TV as the bad guy. A prosecution was pending. Nobody was going to invest in me. I was an extremely bitter young man."

"Has he ever told you this story before?" asked Owen.

Nerys shook her head.

"I'd been earning a very high salary and never had time to spend much so I kept a low profile and worked on the antidote independently. In the media, Bernard Bass was still painting himself whiter than white and bad-mouthing me. I decided to get my own back in a small way. The preparation I was working on was the opposite of Flagrance. It wasn't an attractor, it was a repellent and that's how it smelt. If I could somehow smother Bass's house with that stench I would feel a lot better. Petty, I know, but that's how I felt. But I was having problems with my new product which could not, as yet, be sprayed into the air. It was only effective on contact with water and then it spread through it, eventually forming a thick repulsive-smelling smog resembling sludge-coloured dry ice. It needed a lot of development before people would be able or willing to apply it to themselves. But it was perfect in terms of revenge."

Sanderson lay back on his pillows, a smug expression on his face despite his obvious exhaustion.

"So?" insisted Owen.

"I didn't want to put it in the water supply as I suspected it would be pretty toxic if taken. I didn't want to break in like a common thief. But I had a friend at my local pub, Fred Potts, who worked down the sewers and I kicked around a few ideas with him about getting at the target from below."

Sanderson smiled beatifically.

"The Cox and Rudder was on the river at Hammersmith. There was always a wonderful cross section and a burble of friendly conversation in the bar. Despite all my bad publicity my friends in the Cox stood by me and no-one was more sympathetic than Fred. We'd been pals for a long time, often discussing the effects of chemicals on the environment and sewermen. He was full of entertaining tales of life underground, some horrendous, some funny and I regaled him with stories of Flagrance, B.O. and the campaigns. 'Two ends of the same rainbow, we are, Perfessor,' he used to say."

Sanderson began to laugh which turned into a painful wheeze. Nerys sat him forward and rubbed his back.

"Fred knew everything about the London drains. Not just practical things regarding his work but the whole history since Mediaeval times. 'If I coulda learnt about drains at school I'd'a been a brilliant scholar like you Perfessor,' he told me. 'As it was, I just wasn't interested in nuffing.' In the Cox, Fred told me about the old underground rivers of London: the Fleet, the Tyburn and many others which in earlier times had been sweet-smelling brooks but gradually became no better than drains and disease-carrying open sewers flowing into the Thames."

Sanderson shook his head.

"Back then we thought we had bad pollution but it was worse in those earlier times. Tanneries and dye works discharged their toxic and foul-smelling wastes into the streams and offal and blood from the slaughterhouses often made the rivers run red. There were dead dogs and rats and, of course, human excreta from thousands of latrines."

Nerys shuddered and Owen wrinkled his nose.

"The Great Fire of London should have given the city a fresh start but everybody just returned to their old ways. Cholera, a deadly water-borne disease became rife and then came the Great Stink of eighteen fifty-eight. Traffic on the Thames came to a halt because the paddle steamers were churning excrement to the surface and Parliament debated whether to move upstream to Hampton Court. The man who saved the day was Fred's great hero, Joseph Bazalgette, later Sir Joseph. According to Fred, he should have been canonised."

"So what did he do?"

"He built about a hundred miles of what were termed interceptory sewers under London in perfect Victorian brickwork."

His eyelids drooped.

'They flowed west to east like the Thames, Perfessor, using the gradients and underground rivers to flush the wastes through the system. Quite small, they was, in the west, about four feet high but they increased in diameter as more and more tunnels joined the network. The flow carried the sewage to treatment works east of London. North of the river the High Level Interceptory runs down from Hampstead through Kentish town to the treatment works at Abbey Mills. Then there's two

Middle Levels. One starts at Kilburn and goes through Kings Cross and the other goes down Bayswater and along Oxford Street.'

Sanderson's eyes flipped open.

"Fred drew a map on the table top with his finger dipped in beer. 'There's two low level interceptories,' he said. 'One goes through Kensington, Brompton Road, Piccadilly, through the City to the East End. And here at the Cox we're practically sitting on top of the southern Low Level. That comes from Stamford Brook, goes across Fulham, Chelsea then through to the Victoria Embankment.'"

A musing look entered Sanderson's eye.

"Hundreds of miles of main sewers poured into the interceptories and thousands of miles of local sewers ran into the main sewers and every toilet and every last little drain flushed ultimately into the locals. It was like a vast family tree spreading under the streets of London."

"He's hallucinating," muttered Owen.

"Fred Potts knew all about my work on the odorous antidote. 'What you call this pong, Prof?' he asked. 'It doesn't have a name yet. Because it's so foul, I suppose I could call it Pong I.' He laughed. 'You want to smell a real bad smell I'll take you down there.' He pointed his thumb downward. 'It's against the rules but I will, sometime.' So when I was trying to work out how to get at Bass it was natural my mind should turn to sewers and my friend Fred."

"Very natural," said Owen.

"Shut up, you," hissed Nerys.

"I took him home one night when the pub closed and showed him my scale model of a house with drains flushing through a small perforated container of Pong I into a trough which was the notional sewer below. When I flushed a toilet, also notional, it was pretty spectacular in terms of smoke once the water hit the canister. We crawled out of my basement eyes streaming and coughing our hearts up. But the greatest thing was Fred's reaction to the smell. This case-hardened sewerman, who must have experienced the worst combinations of biological and chemical odours imaginable, thought it was the worst stench ever."

'Phwar! Perfessor! I never smelt nothing like it. But will it go up into the house?'

'It should. Once the smog rises up the drainpipe it should zip through all the S-bends and smother the house.'

We grope through fog to where transparent walls reveal the interior of the model house thick with smoke.

'When it's for real we're gonna need something the size of an oil drum instead of that cocoa tin you got in your model. We'll need breathing apparatus. No problem. Harness and the usual gear. No problem. What we also need is young Charlie Wood who's a dab hand with the remote control and closed circuit TV. That's the problem. Still, Charlie likes money and likes to show off his skills. B.O. Bass lives in Boulton Square; that should impress him. We tell him B.O. will fork out three hundred nicker to have his drains checked on the q.t. Saves all the bother of having the road dug up, see. All computers and electronics these days and spraying polyurethane linings to mend the crumbling old bricks, but the most of it's still Bazalgette's drains, Prof. They're irreplaceable.'

"Fred asked me if it was worth three hundred pounds to get my own back on B.O. When I thought of Pong I penetrating his priceless property in South Kensington it seemed worth every penny. So, I found myself one night donning hard hat, harness and waders in a blue and white van at dead of night just off the Old Brompton Road. What's more, I was being served the traditional hot sweet tea by a scrumptious brunette with limpid blue eyes. In fact, she could have been the spitting image of you, Nerys."

"Me?"

"He's making this up, isn't he?"

"'Who's this?' I asked. 'My daughter, Linda,' he said. 'What's she doing here?' 'Our little jaunt's unofficial. I don't want anyone else in on it. Charlie insists on radio silence but it ain't a healthy place to be if it rains so we need to know and come up double quick.' 'So why can't Charlie let us know?' 'It ain't safe to leave the van unattended.' 'So Linda's going to hop down the sewer and run after us?' Fred grinned. 'Nah! She's going to let us know the way they did before they had radios. She'll lift up the manhole cover and let it drop. We'll hear it.' 'The forecast ain't good,' said Charlie, 'so you better get down there tootsweet. Hold on. I got a video of the bit you're interested in. You better take a quick dekko.'"

Sanderson took a deep breath before continuing.

"We looked at his monitor screen. The video camera traversed the dim tunnels sending shivers up my spine."

'There y'are, Fred, that's the bugger.'

'How high you reckon that outfall is?'

'How high is a Chinaman?'

'Come on, Chas. You're the one who said in, out, no messing and we don't get caught.'

'Reckon that's two foot in diameter. Just right for your oil drum.'

"Fred had decided to tell Charlie what was afoot and he seemed to approve. Soon I was descending a manhole, feeling gingerly for iron rungs set into the sheer wall. 'That wasn't so bad,' I said when we reached the bottom but Fred was lowering his safety lamp down another deeper, blacker hole. He drew the lamp back, nodded and we continued downwards to a tunnel, four feet high and containing a foot of swiftly-flowing noxious fluid. We proceeded, with me attached to Fred by a line, like alpinists in Hades. Walking in the strong current, knees bent to avoid making contact with the slimy brick roof, was excruciating."

Sanderson's eyes closed.

Stumbling on sudden softness underfoot. Fred's voice echoing.

'Steady, Prof. Turn right here.'

Only three feet high. Bend double, ignore the pain in back and thighs. Expanding shadows in torchlight, amplified drippings, nose bent to evil-smelling soup. Fred stops.

'Outfall,' he booms.

Fluid flushes into the tunnel. Past countless spewing outlets till, 'This is the one.'

Heave the canister up to check how it fits with chocks and wadding. Breathing appo on. Pierce the top of the drum like a colander. Too much noise! Fred unperturbed. Tamp it in, firm, immovable. Fred nods again and we start back. A sound reverberates like the knell of doom. I stop. What's happened? Caught red-handed? Fred turns and makes signs with his fingers. What? We go faster. Here's the bigger tunnel. Swifter flowing. Oh my God. I suddenly understand the mime. Pitter-patter, pitter-patter, Linda's dropped the manhole cover. It's raining.

"The phone rang. 'Seen the teletext, Perfessor?' 'No. It's eight in the morning and I only got to bed at four.' 'B.O. Bass is dead, together with a Captain of Industry, some aging film stars and live-in servants all resident in Boulton Square.' 'Good God! How could that be? You and I breathed in the fumes from my model and we're okay. I feel fine. How about you?' 'Terrific. But we gotta get out. I asked Linda what she thought.' 'Linda?' 'Yeah. She's got a good brain. She said maybe it was all right with water but when it was mixed with you-know-what it acted as a catter… a…' 'Catalyst. Jesus. Now I've got to find an antidote for the antidote.'"

His eyes closed again.

'It's spreading eastward, just like you'd expect, along the low level interceptor and all its tributaries. It's waterborne, Dr Sanderson, like cholera only more lethal. I think we should scarper.'

Dr Sanderson! He must be worried.

'Won't that draw attention to ourselves if we run?'

'My mind weren't working that way. I think we got to get out to save our lives.'

'But where?'

'West. It's flowing east but it'll soon start working right through the network, I reckon.'

'Do you really think it's that potent?'

'It's spreading all the time. Look at your teletext.'

"I made the best decision of my life. 'I'll get my lab equipment packed, Fred. Wherever we go I must take it with me. I'll have to find the antidote."

Nerys's face showed alarm.

"People were really dying?"

"Dropping like flies. Fred, Linda and Charlie arrived in separate vehicles, all packed solid. Charlie rushed back and forth squeezing the packed lab equipment into the sewer van and Fred and Linda helped pack my car with my most cherished possessions. 'Good job we're not on the Brompton Road interceptor,' said Fred. 'It'll be the Great Stink all over again. Think I got a whiff already.' 'There'll be a bleeding' stink, all right,' said Charlie. 'Let's blow.'"

'It's eleven o'clock. The pubs are open.'

'You've flipped, Perfessor. We ain't got time to stop for a drink.'

'What I mean is, let's go into the Cox and Rudder and warn everyone and all the other places along the route, pubs, shops, everything.'

'The end is nigh? Come on! Who'll listen?'

'I think we ought to try, Dad.'

"The Cox had a different clientele at that time of day and we didn't know any of the staff. 'The drains!' we shouted. 'They're toxic, they're lethal! Head west!' Then whoosh! Out on the pavement. We worked our way along what used to be the Great West Road."

Sanderson groaned.

"I've never been thrown out of so many places in my life. 'Go west, young bleedin' man,' Charlie kept muttering. So in the end we gave up and our convoy headed out along the M4 motorway. 'Where we going, Dad? Cornwall?' 'I dunno, love.' 'My maternal grandmother lives in West Wales,' I said. 'What about going there?' 'Why not?' So that's how we came to cross the Severn Bridge. I set up my lab in this cottage and tried to work out the antidote.

It was pretty peaceful here but, although contingency plans allowed government and emergency services to be set up outside London, most of the country was in chaos by all accounts. Two months after we'd settled here a chap turned up snooping around. Linda said she felt like killing him because we were about to get married."

"I don't follow that,' said Owen.

"But it turned out all right. Your grandmother wasn't a murderer. His name was Jarvis and he was from MI6. He wanted us to use Pong I to disable other countries because Britain had been put at such a disadvantage politically. As he knew about us, we didn't have much choice. Fred, Charlie and I did Paris, Vienna, New York. They were the famous sewers we were interested in seeing. Not one alligator did we find in New York and there certainly aren't any there now. After that I gave Jarvis the formula and we let him and his henchmen get on with it. At one point they were worried about the third world and Islam gaining the ascendancy but it never happened. We were happy to come back here to the simple life. Fred, who was a widower, married again and Charlie settled down with a local girl and they set up their septic tank emptying services."

"Potts and Wood, of course!"

"For a while I worked on Pong II to try to eradicate Pong I."

"And you never found the right formula?"

"I gave up trying. I was enjoying my new life and had no desire to get back to the old ways. Besides, we were safe here."

"Safe?"

"From the plague."

"But why is it safe here?"

"Because everyone has cesspits. There's no main drainage network. And I have my reserves of Pong I stored in

Aunt Bertha's cellar. That way I have a certain control over the anti-social. Not that they don't always get plenty of warning before I resort to the cesspit method."

Nerys gaped. "And Incomers who are aggressive and throw their weight around are made welcome and put in the Big House. I can just remember that."

"Ah yes. There's always trouble with the water supply and the stopcock's at the end of the long garden, if they but knew. And we turn it on only when we're good and ready. No, we don't need it often but it's a useful resource. I'm amazed you remember the last time."

"Got to disappear a minute," said Owen, rushing out.

An expression of alarm swept Nerys's face. "I think he's gone to get the poison, Grandpa."

"Don't worry." And he told her the true location. "I look to you, Nerys, to take over my responsibilities. Owen will help you more when he's older and wiser. I was thoughtless and irresponsible at his age but since then I've tried to make amends. Your most important task is the maintenance of the pharmacy and keeping the people well. I've taught you both everything I can."

His voice quavered and she kissed him tenderly. He might be a mass murderer but his heart was in the right place.

When Owen returned much later Sanderson was dead.

"Silly old bugger," he muttered. "There's nothing but rusty old lab equipment in the cellar. And I barked my shin. I tried Rhiannon's and Uncle Dai's too. One of his tall tales, I reckon. Oh!"

This last on seeing his grandfather. He stared moodily at the growing crowd outside.

"They'll want to know his last words."

"Yes. He told me what to say."

Owen arched an eyebrow in query.

"Those in positions of authority must serve the needs of the people."

"Doesn't have much of a ring to it. What did he really say?"

She sighed.

"Come on!"

"Not with a bang but an odour."

ARMIES OF MARTYRS

Spring 1899

Dressed in long robes and tall paper mitres, the sacrificial victims walked slowly in single file towards the fires which would consume them.

Hugo, resenting the sun, the lark's happy trill and the scent of burgeoning spring, caught sight of his friend. Everyone looked tall in surplices and high hats but Sebastian was taller still, a beanpole in a cassock.

With a heavy heart and wishing Roberto Valdez had not insisted he come, Hugo left his vantage point on the knoll. He took a zig-zag course towards the crowd, avoiding the mounted soldiery patrolling its edges.

"Let Sebastian see you," Roberto had said. "Let him know that rational men still oppose the Church. Shout out, 'The new century shall be ours' as he passes."

"You want me arrested, too?"

"Not at all! The mob will think you're a hyper-Jesuit. But Seb will know."

Hugo worked his way to the edge of the gangway held open by the Spanish Guard. Their ceremonial helmets and cuirasses glinted in the sun as the condemned walked two or more yards apart in the centre of the wide, grassy path.

Inside the cordon a girl sold flowers from a basket. Her cries grew louder as she drew near. "Buy a flower for the blessed saints. Only a zeta! Lovely flowers. Buy a flower! Only a zeta!"

Hugo, breath held, tried to steel himself to call out as Sebastian approached but the young heretic ahead of him tripped, briefly swayed in an attempt to regain footing, then fell. The line halted.

Two guards sprang forward, whipped off the robe and began beating the victim with truncheons unhooked from their belts. It was a woman and that became more obvious to the mob when they raised her up and forced her to walk on unclothed. The noisy throng began to whistle, cheer and hoot. Some shouted ribald remarks about what might be done with a heretic whore. The young woman stared straight ahead and walked with what dignity bound wrists and haltered ankles allowed.

Hugo saw Seb increase his speed with short, rapid steps.

"Have my robe," he said, once alongside the naked girl and, lifting his cape from his neck with both tied hands, swirled it over his head. With long, haltered limbs making him look like a giant manacled spider, Sebastian let it fall over her shoulders with a neat sideways step.

The crowd howled at losing their sport. Three Guards converged on Sebastian and took turns to beat him systematically about the face, head, shoulders and limbs. Meanwhile, the girl, now ignored, had murmured, "Thank you" and carried on to her fate, no longer exposed.

Sebastian was made to stand, to walk. He moved on, his thin gangly body milk-white, face swollen, nose bloody but head held high. Hugo had no problem now with his task. It came spontaneously. "The new century shall be ours!"

"Thanks to the magic of science," said Seb in a strong voice. The flat of a sword slapped his buttocks causing a delicate line of blood to appear but Sebastian smiled and Hugo suddenly felt better for coming. But he could never stomach the burnings and turned, intending to get away without drawing attention to himself.

A tap on the shoulder made his heart lurch. Turning back, expecting to see a snarling Spanish Guard, he found the flower girl at his shoulder.

"Hugo Palmer?" At his nod, she said, "Follow me."

The girl walked fast back towards Salisbury. They passed a variety of busy stalls. Not all citizens wished to rush to the pyres. Many felt happier buying holy trinkets and poor reproductions of relics. Others indulged themselves with candies, oranges and hot pies rather than see people burn at the stake.

The girl stopped at a stall selling religious paintings.

"Look at the pictures a minute," she said and disappeared behind the canvas and lath construct protecting the wares with a roof and three walls.

John Constable's famous painting *Salisbury Cathedral with Virgin and Angels* was most represented. The cheapest reproductions were three pesetas; tiny, frameless monochromes, badly printed. The best were large, in colour, framed and beyond most people's pockets at two or three hundred pesetas. The quality was improved enough in these for Hugo to admire the wonderful swirl of Constable's clouds supporting the holy figures over the great spire.

"You interested in art, Mr Palmer?" said a broad Wiltshire voice.

Hugo turned to the burly, black-bearded man at his shoulder.

"Very. And science. You're the proprietor?"

"Yes. I'm obsessed by art but where the Scientific Network's concerned, you might call me fanatic. I've a message for you. It'll be easier if you come into Salisbury when the Holy Day is over. Buy something unframed as excuse."

After studying the work on show, Hugo chose a nicely

executed etching of *The Light of the World* by Holman Hunt.

"A man of taste. Bring that to my workshop this evening and I'll frame it for you. Ten zetas in all. John Finch, the carpenter, in Joiners Row."

Hugo parted with the pesetas. "Who produces this work?"

"The good stuff comes from northern Europe. We import all kinds of things through Fishguard," said Finch softly. "A Scot named Edison does the high quality printing for us. You'll meet him should you agree to fill Sebastian's shoes."

Hugo smiled bleakly. "You've chosen a good day to make the offer."

"This is what we put up with," said John Finch, handing over a smudgy handbill from a litter of printed material on the cellar table.

'GRAND AUTO-DA-FÉ,' Hugo read. 'Following the Great Storm and loss of crops last autumn, 300 HERETICS TO BE BURNT ALIVE, on Salisbury Plain on Saint Francis Xavier's Day, 7th April 1899. This ACT OF FAITH shall prevent such occurrence ever again.'

"They give themselves such airs with their rich lifestyles, their Latin and their boasts of great learning," said Alfonso, one of several sitting at the table, "yet they're superstitious as their slaves, the near-naked tribes we hear of in their blessed Spanish America."

"And they can't even print good clean copy," said Nicholas, a young blonde boy with the beginnings of a moustache.

"Were there really three hundred burnt today?" asked Hugo.

"No," said John. "I doubt they took many more than a

hundred. Sebastian went around the countryside warning people to lie low."

"And got caught in the act?"

"No. He was abnormally tall, that's all, so desperate were they for so-called heretics. There were people in that procession today with squints and limps, those their only transgressions. Housewives declared witches because they made cough cures from herbs for their families had been taken and several women who could read and write, an ungodly thing for a female. Others had upset their peers and been denounced out of neighbourly spite. It'd be a farce but for a hundred tragedies. Still, I suppose it's as dangerous in London."

"Perhaps but I'm not burnt like Sebastian. Still, you probably know as much of London matters as me through Valdez's contact."

"My contact plays everything close, only tells me what I need to know."

"That sounds like one of Roberto's, all right," sighed Hugo. "That's why that young girl of yours had to take the risk of contacting me at the auto-da-fé. What if I'd not shouted to Seb?"

"It was instructions," shrugged Finch. "A personal test, perhaps, or an attempt to stop traitors from preying upon us. Certainly, they abound. But here you're among friends."

"Good. But it didn't help Seb. As well as being a friend of many years, he was important to the Scientific Network. Why couldn't you save him?"

"Too well guarded and too great a danger that the rescuers would be taken or recognised. We have to live here. There's nothing to be gained if we run. Once, we got armed horsemen from Wales to sweep in and snatch our people to safety but the Guard are ready now with horsemen of their own."

"What did Sebastian do here?"

"We're one of the staging posts between London and the West Country, and sometimes Wales. He helped us with the Network but really was on his way to Europe, through Fishguard, to liaise with potential allies; Prussia, Russia, the Netherlands. Did you know they're generating electricity in Brussels to run trams?"

"Who told you that?"

"Seb. He'd been there, ridden on one! The Dutch Calvinists run their trams almost within sight of the Spanish Netherlands to the south, where to experiment with electricity is to be in league with the devil and merits the death penalty!"

"It's a mad world," muttered Hugo.

"Anyway, he was waiting here for his interpreter when we learnt the fellow'd been denounced and detained in London. That's how Maria got involved."

"Maria?"

"The flower girl. My sister's child. She's lived here as my daughter since her parents burnt. She volunteered to be the new interpreter."

"Not just a flower girl, then."

"No, not just a simple Wiltshire lass. She's fluent in five or six languages. But I worry people will find out she can read and write and the opportunity for her to travel to places where it's no sin seemed too good to turn down. Maria agrees to be your interpreter if you take Sebastian's place but we need to know."

"It's a big step for a messenger. For that's all I've been till now."

"Yes. You'd be a kind of diplomat, pulling strings, getting support for us against the Faith."

"Roberto never had a chance to discuss it with me but it's clearly what he intended." Hugo paused then sighed. "So I'll have to agree."

"Good! We'll drink to your success. Joachim, draw some ale while I show our guest Hugo some of the art stock never out on open view."

Smiling broadly, Finch handed over a good reproduction of Hogarth's *Cardinal in Sun and Shade*. The cleric, dressed in traditional red robes and biretta, sat inside a window, his face distorted, one side smiling in sun, the dark half scowling. The hand in sunshine was raised in benediction over a groaning board of rich provisions. The hand in shadow fondled the exposed breast of a prostitute while beyond in dark corners rats fled a torturer's dungeon.

Hugo smiled grimly. "No wonder Hogarth burned."

"He hanged. For treason. Philip the Fifth protected him, enjoying the Church's discomfort for a while, but when Hogarth began to lampoon the Bourbons and compare palace wealth with dereliction on the streets, he lost his support."

"Suicidal."

"But you've got to admire him. No scientist but one of our many martyrs."

"You should be a historian, John Finch, an academic, not a carpenter."

John laughed. "Don't know how you got your learning, Hugo, but no ordinary Englishman gets a formal education round here. I'm a self-taught man."

All turned anxiously as the lantern suspended from the ceiling rocked and the candles guttered with the opening of the door.

"Ah, here's Maria. She's self-taught, too."

"That's only part true. I owe a great deal to my fathers. This one," she smiled, kissing John, "and my other father."

"Hugo's agreed to take Sebastian's place."

"Good. I'll get my cloak and we'll take a walk and discuss our plans. There's much he needs to know."

"Is it safe to walk abroad at night in Salisbury?"

John Finch clapped Hugo on the shoulder with a grin. "Don't worry, Maria knows Salisbury inside out. She'll take care of you."

"So Sebastian's death didn't put you off," said Maria.

An obnoxious stench of singed flesh wafted through the city's streets, blown from the Plain on a strong northwest wind.

"The injustices appal me. Experiments with electricity or chemicals aren't sorcery. Scientists are rational people with healthy enquiring minds who may discover things of benefit to all mankind. But having no scientific bent myself, supporting the Network is the only contribution I'm able to make."

"Seb and I agreed to travel as man and wife. It wouldn't be seemly for a single woman to travel as an independent companion. He'd agreed that our relationship would be chaste. Are you willing to travel under the same conditions?"

"I am, providing it doesn't get back to my fiancée in London. Or perhaps a message through Roberto assuring Catherine of my fidelity might be better."

"Ah, Catherine. What's her other name?"

"Diaz. What's yours? Not really Finch, I take it."

"Wheatstone."

"Related to Charles Wheatstone, the martyr?"

"Yes. My grandfather. I never met him. My father changed the family name but somebody discovered and betrayed us."

"So you have ample reason to support the Network."

"Yes. As to Catherine, perhaps saying nothing at all about your travelling companion would avoid planting the seed of doubt."

Hugo inspected her smooth, young face closely in the light of the moon. "Are you always so wise?"

The two horses plodded resignedly. Cold rain blew under Hugo's hat-brim and sluiced down his cheeks.

"How will we know when we're in Wales?" he shouted over the wind.

Maria had no opportunity to reply. Horsemen rode out of the curtain of rain and surrounded them.

"What have we here, then?" demanded a rough, accented voice.

"*Ffrindiau*," said Maria, "*ffrindiau o Loegr*."

A torrent of speech followed, totally incomprehensible to Hugo. A horseman took Maria's rein and began to lead her away.

"What are they saying? What are they saying?"

"We're over the border. They'll lead us south to *Caerdydd*, Cardiff. There's a Network man there."

A bearded, villainous-looking rider came and grasped Hugo's rein but appeared less threatening when he grinned broadly and raised his streaming hat.

"Friends from England, eh?" said the villain. "*Croeso*. Welcome to Wales."

"How was the cawl?" asked Thomas Edison.

A man of about fifty, his accent was almost as weird as those of the Welshmen, due to having a Scottish father and a Dutch mother, according to Maria.

The broth tasted wonderful as did the bread, the cake, the ale and Hugo said as much.

"You need to see everything going on here so we'll travel to Fishguard by way of the mines and industrial complex expanding all along this south coast. But first I'll show you the big guns down on the Cardiff waterfront."

"Why go to Fishguard when we have a perfectly serviceable port here?"

"Cardiff's being used for commerce but it's not completely safe yet. Bristol's only across the estuary. That's where our guns point. We're building steamships at Milford Haven while Pembroke and Swansea are developing into busy ports, too, but my workshops are at Fishguard and I want you to see them before you sail. We want Europe to know that we also have scientific innovation to offer."

"Is it true they have gas lamps in Prussia?" asked Maria.

"Yes. Siemens and Swan are working wonders with electricity," he said, grinning wolfishly, "but my electric lamps are better."

"Arc lamps?" Hugo asked.

"No better than that. At least, they will be. We need big generators for whole communities but an ordered society is necessary for that and a prosperous one. And that may be possible if Hugo successfully negotiates with our allies. Then we'll take Bristol. Our friends in the west will sweep on eastwards and the northern Welsh will secure Liverpool, the Wirral and link up with the Scots. Spanish England will be overrun."

"Are you sure I'm the right man?" stammered Hugo.

"You are," Thomas smiled. "Don't worry. You'll receive detailed instructions. And Maria is the right woman. The whole operation would be impossible without her talents. Never forget that."

They held out for three weeks. A kiss on the electric tram on their way to a Brussels art gallery was the turning point. Hugo looked into Maria's eyes. Drawing a deep breath, she returned his gaze.

"Let's go back," she whispered and they both climbed down from the streetcar and returned to their hotel room in breathless haste.

"The last three weeks have been hell," said Hugo, as he rolled back across the bed, "a wonderful, on the brink of heaven kind of hell but nevertheless… We must get married then we won't have to live this lie any longer."

"That might be difficult. Everyone thinks we're married already."

"There must be somewhere with a discreet cleric – Catholic, Lutheran, Calvinist, I don't mind which – willing to make an honest woman of you."

Maria laughed. "They all want commitment, a month or more to learn your catechism or some other mumbo-jumbo, so they feel you're in their power. Let's be rational, enjoy our love while it lasts and continue to show our conventional married face to the world. And then, what about Catherine? Do you suddenly no longer love her?"

"I'm totally besotted by you."

"Not good enough," she laughed. "Soon you'll be besotted by someone else and I'll be disregarded like poor Catherine. So the present situation suits us fine."

"So cruel," he whispered. "I've never thought of you as cruel, always kind."

Smiling, they fell into each other's arms again.

Summer 1900

"This information could be relayed by courier, Hugo," said Thomas, mopping his brow. "Why put your life in jeopardy? According to Raul Lambert the Network's under great pressure in London. Suspicion is rife. Even your powerful guardian's at risk."

"Roberto? But as Bishop of London… Surely not."

"Let's say he's having to tread very carefully."

"In truth, the political information could go by courier but I've got to attend to a personal matter with Roberto, face to face."

"And you're not marrying Maria before you leave Fishguard, after all? She said that in Brussels you wanted to marry immediately."

"On reflection, it's better to formally end a previous liaison first."

"Tell the other young lady to her face? You're a brave man. The kind of ceremony you could have here wouldn't count as marriage to the likes of your devout Catholic fiancée or her family."

"Please don't denigrate Catherine because of her religion and upbringing. She's kind and considerate, sensitive and vulnerable. That's why I must tell her, not let her feel thrown off like a discarded shoe."

"Well, ask Maria if she has any important news to impart before you go."

"Important? What do you mean?"

Hugo stared at Thomas's bland and secretive smile and had a sudden inkling of what he might be inferring.

"Not…? A child? She wouldn't tell you before me, surely."

"Of course not. Maybe a man over fifty is inclined to be more observant."

But Hugo was gone, running back to their rooms at the Royal Oak.

"Gwilim will conduct the ceremony," said Thomas.

Gwilim Jenkin was the villainous-looking rider they'd

met on first reaching Wales. Though grateful to Edison for arranging permanent accommodation for them before his departure, Hugo was unable to stop himself saying, "Couldn't you find somebody more suitable?"

"Gwilim's a bard of great standing," Thomas replied. "Poets are highly regarded in this society and often perform important official functions."

"He doesn't look anything like a poet to me."

Maria kissed him and smiled. "How many have you met?"

In the event, Gwilim performed his task well, beard trim, face solemn, neat in black frock-coat, stock and high collar. Standing before the ancient dolmen of Pentre Ifan under a scorching sun, Maria and Hugo made their vows.

"Roberto is constantly watched," said Raul Lambert. "He suggests you don't go and see him but give me the information you've gathered in Europe. As a member of his staff at Fulham Palace, I can pass it on when it's safe."

They strolled beside the Thames hoping for a breath of air, relief from the continuing hot weather, but it was low water and the river stank.

"That's no problem," said Hugo. "The invasion is planned. Some spoke of next spring but they're being over-optimistic. There's too much to organize. The Prussians and Dutch will take part in the drive from Wales and the West but won't make a seaborne landing elsewhere. They'll have ships visible off the coast, tying up a lot of the enemy forces in the east and south but won't land unless our forces can sweep right across the country. Unfortunately, I don't think they will. Edison seems to think we can hold a line as far east as Portsmouth in the first push."

"Why not take London, the whole island? We keep hearing what advanced technology the Calvinists have. Surely it would be easy for them?"

"It's true the alliance now has ironclad horseless carriages as well as ships. Edison's working on a fantastic electrical communications system and Marconi says, eventually, people will be able to send messages to ships out of sight at sea."

"Then efforts should be coordinated to secure the whole mainland. To stop short will simply give the enemy time to regroup and hit back."

"It's a compromise. Many don't want to wage war. Ferranti and Marconi see modern technology as a bringer of peace. They dream of an ordered existence, a society where modern inventions will provide a comfortable life for everyone."

"They'll have to change society first. Can't they see that?"

"Edison and Maxim do. And Vladimr Ulyanov in Russia. He calls himself Lenin now and plans to overthrow the Romanovs. According to him, the country is even more backward than England, the workers abjectly poor and deprived. When called upon, he claims, the down-trodden will rise up and they'll eventually enjoy a rich lifestyle with electricity for all, modernized industry, fair distribution of the fruits of the earth, an economically successful land."

"A tall order considering the vast extent of the country."

"Yes. But with backing from independent Europe and given political success, he pledges to help Britain fight for freedom so the Holy Roman Empire can be threatened from both west and east. We felt justified in offering to help the Bolsheviks shake off the yoke of the Tsarists and their fat priests."

Raul sucked air through his teeth. "A rash promise. We could see death staring whole battalions in the face. Our battalions."

"Prussia and the Netherlands will provide the bulk of

the troops but I had to agree to some commitment on our part. It seemed worth it. The Papal states could in the end become a weak enclave under constant blockade."

"Good. You've made great progress, Hugo. Everything will be passed on to Bishop Valdez. There's no need for you to risk seeing him."

"As my guardian, I need to discuss a personal matter with him. About my engagement to his niece. There'll be no risk."

"Catherine Diaz? Her father's pulling a lot of political strings lately. Well… If it's definitely non-political I'll make an appointment with the Bishop for confession. But bear in mind that these are no longer entirely private."

"Father forgive me for I have sinned."

Roberto was merely a shadow behind the screen. The tension in his voice told Hugo that others were listening.

His worst confession was fornication. He assured Roberto that though no longer able to marry his niece, he cared about her, had written every week while away, still liked and respected her and must tell her so.

"Better not to subject her to such pain, my son. Leave London now."

"Yes, when this last message is delivered."

"I shall give you Absolution," his guardian whispered. Hugo had to strain his ears to hear. "Heed my advice. Leave London immediately. Don't return to your lodgings. Belongings can be replaced, lives cannot."

Outside, he glimpsed Raul disappearing round a corner. Hugo called and ran to catch up. Two men stepped out of a doorway into his path.

"Mind where you're going, fellow!" said one, stamping

on his instep and buffeting his head. The other twisted his arm painfully behind his back.

After being bundled into a carriage, Hugo saw out of the corner of his eye Raul reappear round the corner, hover for a second then flee.

The only replies to his questions were vicious blows to the face.

They travelled westward and eventually drew into the drive of the fine Kew mansion of Fernando Diaz. Once in the stable yard, Hugo was pulled and pummelled through a side door, dragged down some stairs and thrown into a cellar. Both his captors hustled in after. They gave him the kind of systematic beating which Sebastian had suffered before his death.

Breathless, Hugo shouted, "What is this? Why? Why?"

They beat him all the harder.

Despite the bright blue of Fishguard Bay, Maria felt a wave of dread flow through her at the sight of Thomas toiling up the hill, leading his horse in the blistering sun.

He hitched the horse under the shade of a tree in the garden and walked slowly towards the cottage. Maria poured water for both man and horse.

"I've news from Raul Lambert's courier," said Thomas, taking his cup with gratitude and insisting on carrying the water bucket to his mount. "Not good, I'm afraid. The London Network no longer exists. Bishop Valdez is in the Tower. Lambert's been taken, too."

"And Hugo?"

"We don't know," sighed Edison, mopping his brow. "Probably captured. He could be lying low but… I'm sorry, Maria. Don't be too optimistic. Of course, you'll always have support from me, from all of us. On the brighter side, the courier came by way of Salisbury. Everyone there, including your uncle, is well and busy recruiting."

"For the Network?"

"For the Army. The Wiltshire Volunteers, John calls them. Maybe they'll be sweeping through London before long and save Hugo."

The heat and the burgeoning child within her already weighed Maria down. The bad news and the thought that her uncle, her only living relative and substitute father, as well as neighbours and childhood friends might be killed or maimed in battle made her feel sick and faint.

Thomas took her arm and led her into the cool cottage interior.

After the beating Hugo was left to rot.

When recovered enough, he crawled to the faint glimmer of light from a ventilation grille, hauled himself up and found a worm's-eye-view of grass blades translucent in the evening sun. Beyond, shadows stretched across a lawn which sloped down to the banks of the Thames. Hugo and Catherine had spent idyllic summer afternoons rowing upstream with a picnic and a mandolin. If only he could reach the boathouse but there was no way out.

Up in one corner, the lid of a coal-hole proved immovable and, anyway, too small to squeeze through. The slope of coal beneath seemed the least uncomfortable place to sit or sleep. He was reduced to relieving himself in the opposite corner.

Each morning a little light came through the grille with the dawn chorus. The larger, more brutal, captor brought the occasional meal, invariably stale bread and old cheese on a dented metal tray with water in a tin mug. Any questions brought forth a cosh and a bludgeoning to add to Hugo's existing bruises and lacerations.

On the third evening his captors came and thrashed

him once more before dragging him from the stinking, stifling cellar to stand before Fernando Diaz.

Diaz lolled on a brocade sofa, his stomach bulging beneath a bright yellow cummerbund and embroidered waistcoat. Hugo stood before him blinking, struggling to remain upright. Blood streaked his shirt-front and he could feel his left eye swelling.

"I must apologise that you've had to wait so long for my return."

"Don't worry, the Diaz hospitality has been superb."

The two ruffians moved in, fists raised, but Diaz waved them back.

"Why am I treated like this? Do you care so much that your daughter will no longer be marrying a man without fortune or property?"

"Though not overjoyed that you're rejecting my daughter, hurting her, that's not the reason you're here. As to money and property, you were acceptable because of your family connections. I expected a descendant of Guy Fawkes, our most famous and longest serving parliamentarian, to be both trustworthy and patriotic."

Hugo thought Diaz's own patriotism merely protected his élite position as an overseas plantation owner. The sweat of unseen slaves maintained his lifestyle and provided high profits for funding government and buying favours.

"I, not you, shall tell Catherine of your betrayal. Of her, of your country, of the Faith. My brother-in-law, your guardian, Bishop Roberto Salvatori Valdez," he pulled his mouth into a moue of contempt, "has been under suspicion for some time. Expect no help from him. He's in the Tower of London awaiting the arrival of a high-ranking Dominican of the Inquisition from Madrid. You won't meet but you'll both suffer. He'll be singing soon and so will you."

"I've nothing to sing of."

Diaz gave a mirthless laugh. "Nothing to sing about? Did it never occur to you that Spain and Holy Church have their own spies in Europe? All we need now are a few more names and dates. Is there anything you wish to confess meantime, in the interests of making your life easier in days to come?"

"Nothing."

"Very well. We already know a great deal about the plans of the Battalions of the Devil but I'm sure you'll fill in the detail. You can expect the rack as encouragement, the red hot poker and much, much more. You'll sing and you'll crave death. Eventually, that craving will be granted, too, either the fire or the gallows. Tonight, you can enjoy the comparative comfort of my cellars."

Back in the darkness of the cellar Hugo slumped down onto the coal.

He drifted off to sleep until the key turning in the lock awoke him. Catherine's mother stood silhouetted in the doorway holding aloft a lantern and beckoning. Coal cascaded around his feet as Hugo stood up. She led him outside and down to the boathouse where Catherine had manoeuvred a rowing boat alongside the landing stage.

A rosy glow still flushed the western sky. The gleaming river smelt of mud, a fast incoming tide flowing past. With luck, the boat would be carried way upstream before the oars were needed.

"Thank you. Will you give me a good push towards midstream?"

"We're all leaving, Mr Palmer," Mrs Diaz replied softly and pointed to three grips stowed in the stern.

Though taken aback, Hugo extended his hand to help her into the craft. Using an oar, he pushed them out as far as possible and they began to drift upstream.

He reached to kiss Catherine's hand.

"Your face, Hugo," she whispered, touching his swollen cheek gently.

A water bird hooted nearby but no sound or movement came from the grounds of the Diaz mansion.

"We should be safe," said Mrs Diaz. "My husband's gone to a political meeting and his louts are with him. Only my servants are in the house. I know you're injured but row upstream, if that's possible, Mr Palmer, past Isleworth Ait and moor at the landing stage beside the ferryman's cottage."

They slid quietly past the island and moored. The swarthy young ferryman, appearing immediately, muttered, "Barney" and helped them ashore.

After hustling them into his sparse, plank-floored dwelling, he examined Hugo's bruised face. "I'll bathe that. What's all this filth?"

"Coal-dust and blood mainly."

Barney rummaged in one of the grips from the stern of the boat.

"Right. That shirt off, good wash and this one on."

The water was cold and stung his skin.

"I'm off to sink your boat," said Barney. "Shan't be long."

"I don't know how to thank you ladies," said Hugo once the ferryman left.

"We had little choice. You must read these," said Catherine's mother.

There were two letters, one from Roberto and one from Raul.

Roberto begged him to escort his sister and her daughter to Portsmouth, there embark for the Continent and accompany them for their entire journey to safety with cousins in Geneva.

"Are you really at risk from your own husband and Catherine from her father?"

"Roberto is denounced. My husband may be under pressure from his so-called political friends to prove his complete loyalty by denouncing us."

"Surely this country's run by demonic madmen," muttered Hugo.

Raul's letter told of the arrangements for their journey and concluded, 'At present, I believe myself to be undetected and shall inform everyone in Wales of what has happened and of the likely long delay before your return. Please try to expedite the spring offensive while in Europe for the sake of all those recently taken who might be saved.'

They sat on Barney's hard wooden chairs, the only kind he had, until a covered cart arrived in the small hours.

"I'll make the ladies comfy inside," Barney told Hugo. "You sit up top with Josh, the driver. He's a Network man, too."

As the horse clopped steadily along, Josh said, "We'll cross the river at Kingston Bridge and I'll drop you for the first stagecoach to Portsmouth. If we just kept on beside the river we'd come to Hampton Court. Henry the Eighth had the right idea, eh? Have our own church, our own ways. I always feel English. Don't you?"

"Bit of both really but don't side with the powers that be as you must realise."

"That Philip o' Spain was dead lucky with his Armada and the weather set fair. No chance, our lot. Before that he wanted to marry our Elizabeth, you know. She wasn't having any and even if she'd married she wouldn't have. She would've denied him his conjugals, I reckon, and serve the bugger right."

Hugo gave a taut smile.

"We should have had our own monarchs. Instead we've had all these Spaniards."

That was true. Elizabeth had fled to Ireland but had no heirs who might challenge the usurpers. Philip the Second of Spain became Philip the First of England and his line and its Catholic administrators remained in control.

But Hugo was more concerned with his own succession and wished he were heading for Wales and Maria instead of Portsmouth and the Continent. And he had yet to tell Catherine of his marriage.

February 1902

Dear Maria,

It grieves me to be away and miss young Hugo's first birthday but I'm sending a handsome present by carrier and some French perfume for you.

Negotiations, as usual, are hanging fire. I wish you were my interpreter picking up the nuances. Occasionally, the Dutch and Prussians are convinced that they need our little island to threaten the Holy Roman Empire from the west, other times they think we're irrelevant. For my part, I'm sure our support is essential and will enable the Allies to run an effective blockade once hostilities begin. Their negotiators insist that first they must be certain of support on the Russia borders. Only then will they help secure the British mainland. I've no idea when that may be.

I recently saw Gustave Courbet's *The Stonebreakers* in Dresden, a brilliant painting, stunningly executed. My interpreter, complete with walrus moustache, was no substitute for having you with me.

How I miss you and long for you, through every day and every night.

With all my love and longing,
Hugo

May 1905

Dear Catherine,

It grieves me to be away for young Hugo's birthday again. I'm sending him a handsome present by carrier as well as some Russian dolls for you. Each one opens to reveal a smaller one inside.

A courier informs me that my guardian, your uncle, Roberto, is dead. I grieve for him. The only consolation is that death must have been a release after their long sufferings in the Tower. Please break the news as gently as possible to your mother.

Negotiations with Lenin move on apace. The Prussian and Lithuanian armies have met halfway in northern Poland and stand poised to invade Russia. Dutch, British and Danish troops are ready to disembark at both Archangel and St Petersburg. The unrest following the shooting of strikers in Siberia has forced the Tsar to relent and grant a constitution with a Duma but this parliament is useless according to Lenin and the Revolution will go ahead. I am excited but apprehensive.

Hugs and kisses to the children.
With all my love and longing,
Hugo

Autumn 1909

They came to a halt within thirty miles of London. John Finch had expressed his frustration with a string of broad-vowelled swear words.

Crippen, their Commanding Officer, had been hit and a man named Paisley took over the Wiltshires, calling himself Colonel. Hugo, designated Captain, had acquired considerable military experience with the regiment in Russia but had not insisted on his right to lead. This he now regretted. Paisley turned out to be a fanatic who treated all suspected Catholics with appalling ruthlessness, shooting and hanging men, women and children and burning their dwellings. Hugo's anger, threats and pleas for the sake of future reconciliation had no effect. Added to which, the man was making basic mistakes and putting the unit at risk.

Until now, the advance had been slow but effective thanks to their armoured cars and lethal machine guns. The vehicles were useless cross-country but made steady progress along the rutted stagecoach roads. Crippen assigned infantry to form a kind of bow wave flowing out into the fields and woodlands either side of the advance. Some of the opposition fought with fanaticism but there were numerous others who gave themselves up, wishing to change sides. They were passed to the rear to be vetted, kitted out and pointed in the right direction. The army was swelling as they progressed.

Now they were stopped. Paisley had insisted on crossing the Thames by way of the narrow bridge at Marlow. Hugo had donned his helmet and sprinted to the front to tell him they should stay north of the river. Its meanderings would mean having to cross and recross it, slowing their progress even further. Bridges were few and far between and could offer the enemy opportunities for ambush.

Paisley wouldn't listen. Their cars became pinned down and were temporarily abandoned.

Hugo sat in the middle of a small hollow full of fallen, toast-coloured leaves. Thick yew trees screened him from bullets crackling and whining from the direction of Cookham. Surely he'd become too old for this sort of adventure, a man of thirty-five with two wives and five children.

He mused upon his weaknesses. Caring too much about hurting others had turned him into a bigamist. Unfortunately, Catherine could not be dissuaded from naming their firstborn Hugo. Sometimes he'd imagine the two namesakes meeting in later life and arguing, 'No, I'm Hugo Palmer!'

Paisley was bellowing. On the order they should advance. He would probably get them all killed. Thankfully, with Edison's help, Maria would care for Hugo and their daughter Charlotte. Catherine and her mother's family in Switzerland would do the same for his other offspring.

Resignedly, Hugo rose, hefted his rifle and crouched to make himself as small a target as possible when emerging from cover.

"Stand by," called Paisley in a loud growl. "Advance!"

A hand grabbed Hugo's ankle.

"Where you going, Captain?" said a Wiltshire voice and he looked down to find Joachim grinning up at him.

"Paisley's a dangerous idiot, Jo," whispered Hugo, "but I can't desert."

"We're not deserting. We're waiting for John and Alfonso's pincer movement to bear fruit."

"Did Paisley have the sense to order that?"

"No. They took it on themselves, unscrewed a machine gun from an assault car. Young Nick's carrying it on his back."

Small arms fire came from up ahead followed by the rat-tat-tat of a Maxim and men screaming. Peering from cover, Hugo and Joachim saw John Finch, Alfonso and several others saunter down from the previously lethal copse. Nick, now a tall and broad-shouldered man, followed with the machine gun across his shoulders.

"All clear!" shouted John. "I think we'll appoint Hugo

as our new commander. Providing he undertakes to follow Crippen's strategy."

"What's happened to Paisley?"

"The Colonel got shot."

A knowing smile played around Finch's lips, making Hugo suspect that Paisley's death might not have involved the enemy.

Camped on Hounslow Heath, local people plied them with food and ale.

"For pity's sake don't let the men get drunk, John."

"No," said Finch. "I doubt they'll have any more fighting but they should enter London looking like heroes, not a rabble."

Next day, in slanting golden sun, the lines of armoured vehicles advanced along King Philip Street towards the ancient Parliament building.

Hugo stood in the Wiltshires' leading car with John Finch and waved and smiled at the cheering crowds.

Ten years had passed since Sebastian's death. As he eyed the noisy throng, twenty and thirty deep, Hugo felt a twinge of doubt. To his mind, they looked not so very different from the mob which had taunted the condemned on Salisbury Plain on that far-off St Francis Xavier's Day.

DARLING STARLINGS

Ed had already begun lumbering towards the newly-landed vessel when dense black streams began to pour from its interior like polluting smoke. The dark stains merged and spread across the sky. Although it was expected, a groan went up from the group assembled by the transparent tunnel under the flags and bunting.

"Damn starlings," hissed Ed into his helmet headset but he kept walking. He had made the entry for the last five years, ever since Chaz had been lost, and he always remained unruffled.

When he was halfway to the vehicle the main hatch slid open. This was also expected.

"Min hatch open," muttered Ed.

Only he was to communicate at this stage, the rest must maintain silence. He always made the most of it.

"Steps extending."

Then, "Reached the foot of the stairway."

"About to climb."

The onlookers sighed silently, rolled their eyes upward or gritted their teeth.

As Ed concentrated on placing his feet on the ladder, somebody appeared in the hatchway. Everyone but Ed could see the figure. In theory, they kept their intercom silence. In practice, Ed heard the sudden, simultaneous intake of breath of about forty people.

He looked up in alarm but the steps were steep and high. He could see nothing.

"What is it?" he asked. "Break silence!"

A cacophony of variations on "Somebody in the hatchway" bounced around his helmet.

"Stop!" he yelled. "Fay, you tell me."

"Somebody's appeared in the hatchway," said the Administrator, "small as far as I can tell and not wearing a suit."

"Not Chaz?"

"No."

"What's it wearing?"

"Trousers and a tee-shirt."

"I've got an enlarger on it," said another voice which Ed recognised as Fay's partner, Jon. "There's writing on the tee-shirt. It says, 'I love Eta – Seventh Heaven'."

"I'm going on."

Ed continued his slow climb. Before he reached anywhere near the top, the figure stepped to the edge of the hatch and looked about.

The voice was young and female. It rang out clear in the still air.

"Er, hello. Where is this, please?"

Ed was nearly there. Famed for his laid-back approach to life, he peered over the highest stair and said, "Oh, hi. How in space did you get to be aboard this autoshut?"

As he had his helmet on, only members of the group heard him.

Reaching the top, he removed his helmet and repeated the question.

"Well, quite by accident, really."

"I believe you."

"Is this Earth?"

She was Tessa McTaggart, aged about fourteen years, from the planet Eta and disappointed to learn that she had landed on Tau.

"We'll call you Tess," said Ed.

He did his limited inspection of the shuttle with the

usual negative result and they both clambered down the ladder to the ground.

Fay put a protective arm around the girl.

"There are cages and cages of birds on there," said Tess.

"Just cages now," said Ed. "The birds have flown."

"And kilos of kippers."

"Kippers! Did you see any kippers, Ed?"

"Can't say I did."

"Would you know one if you saw one?" enquired Jon. "I wouldn't."

"There were crates and crates of them. I ate an awful lot but there's still plenty left."

"Full of protein and vitamins, we could have done with those," said Fay.

"Couldn't you go back?" asked Tess.

"It'd take too long. That's how we lost Chaz."

Nobody moved and the girl looked questioningly at Fay.

"We're waiting for the hatch to shut and the craft to take off, Tess. The Annual Shuttle, The Ansh, isn't what it was but it's still the major event of the year. You'll find life is pretty quiet on Tau. I hope you won't get bored."

Soon the hatch closed, the engines fired and the vast ship rose with a roar.

"Definitely no more kippers," said Tess.

"What do they taste like?" asked Ed.

"Very dry and salty but there was plenty of water on board. It was automatically dispensed for the birds. And birdseed."

Suddenly the massed starlings on the spaceport buildings rose as one. With a whirring of wings and a communal twittering they blotted the sun from the sky. Abruptly banking, the black, constantly shifting cloud seemingly paused then set off in an easterly direction. When the vast host had passed, sunlight glinted once more on the glassy roofing of the Far Western Sector and silence returned.

The assembled administrators and dignitaries gravitated towards the transparent tunnel for the annual Ansh Dinner.

"Here's your first lesson on how to behave on Tau, Tess," said Fay. "Always shut the mesh doors to the outside. It stops the birds getting in."

"Why's that?"

"They eat our food. They'd strip everything. We want to survive, right?"

"Right."

"And if after living on kippers, water and birdseed you start chirping, we'll probably send you outside to live with the starlings."

"Don't be such a horrible tease, Ed."

Tess stared into her monitor screen as the tutor droned on. Tauan history was so dull.

By the time Tau had been discovered, Earth Administration had it all worked out. Hard-working people of even temperament were dispatched in their thousands. Bor-ing. At least Eta had previously had wars, riots, famines and factions. In between had been the golden ages. They were the mind-numbing bits.

Suddenly the video swarmed with starlings. Tess sat up and took notice.

"The coming of the birds marked the end of a golden age on Tau," said the tutor.

This should be more interesting.

"For its entire history Tau had been kept supplied by personnel shuttles. Suddenly contact with Earth was only by way of the annual automatic shuttle. Annual Shuttle Day was still a big occasion but it wasn't quite the same and soon efficient two-way communication broke down.

Supplies which were ordered never arrived. Instead the ships would land with some completely different cargo. It didn't take much to realise that we were getting some other colony's supplies and some other planet must be getting ours."

Tess jabbed her green light.

"Tess?"

"On Eta they got the things they asked for but years and years later when nobody wanted them anymore."

"What sort of things, Tess?"

"Kippers, hot water bottles, haggis, stuff like that."

"I see. Certainly that's comparable to what happened here. Not only did orders arrive years later but they kept coming and in increasing quantities. That's why we're now inundated with starlings."

Their monitors changed to a still of an official Space Service Requisition Form.

Oh-oh, this is going to be just as boring as usual, thought Tess.

"The first request for birds was made when the Administration heeded pleas for something to be done about insects which were creating a great nuisance. They applied for a consignment of garden birds but nothing happened. Then, five years later, out of the blue, the first batch of starlings arrived. It wasn't quite what people wanted. They'd expected robins, wrens, finches. Nevertheless, homesteaders were delighted to have them in their gardens and colonising the trees. It was a new luxury to hear birds and watch them feed. The starlings' greedy antics were considered very funny. Look at your screens and you'll see why."

A scrum of starlings feeding from scraps appeared on the monitors. They manoeuvred, chased, jumped over each other, waddled and skipped, competing for food. Their movements were as fast as a comedy cartoon and Tess laughed out loud. The other pupils sat in stony silence.

"For a while, starlings were very popular. My own great-grandmother, so I'm told, who lived above ground, loved the birds and used to stand at her kitchen window exclaiming, 'Oh, those darling starlings.'"

There were gasps at this admission of awful blasphemy by a direct ancestor.

"Bird tables and feeders appeared in every garden. Starlings were popular."

"We asked for birds on Eta because of the insects", said Tess.

"I had no idea Eta had an insect problem."

"Oh, yes. On Eta there are insects as big as tea plates."

The face of Ben, the tutor, appeared on the screen and his eyes narrowed suspiciously. "Right. So birds thrived and did reduce the insect population. On the next shuttle another consignment of starlings arrived, twice as many as before. Each year more birds arrived in greater and greater numbers. They were automatically released once the ship had landed and there was nothing we could do to stop them entering our skies. Starlings became a plague."

"Wow. I wish we had some back on Eta," said Tess. "I'm sure they'd help in controlling those enormous great insects."

"Will you please not interrupt, Tess, and just record your lesson the same as everyone else."

Tess bent her head over her screen.

"My great-grandmother would have been one of the last to find starlings delightful. They proved to be a very successful species. They colonised this planet with much greater ease than humankind. Soon they were competing with us and having a far more devastating effect upon the crops than the insects they were intended to control. Our Administration kept sending frantic messages saying, 'No more starlings', 'Please send no more birds!', 'Positively no more starlings!', but it made no difference. Still they came and so it continues to this day. How did Tau manage to cope with the threat of birds?"

The monitors indicated green lights everywhere.

"Yes, Joy?"

"They began to grow everything under transparent cover."

"That's right. But there were not enough materials to support the roofings. How was that solved?"

More green lights.

"Ray?"

"They excavated."

"Yes. At first only on a small scale but gradually the canopied areas expanded to ninety per cent of the agricultural land. Then began the incorporation of the dwelling areas for the convenience of the growers and for extra safety. The less people went in and out, the fewer chances for starlings to get inside."

"Sometimes the light system fails," whispered Al who sat next to Tess.

"Why's that?"

"The wind generators stop generating."

"Oh?"

"No wind."

"So what happens in class?"

"We put our hands up."

"Stop that talking," snapped Ben. "Now I'm going to show you a map. This is the civilised extent of our planet. The bulk of it is under transparency or so-called glass, a tribute to our parents and grandparents who worked hard and improvised to give us all protection. There are still parts of the canopies formed from greenhouses, conservatories and old solar transporters. They're still solidly built and safe."

A cursor activated on the far left of the viewer.

"Here's where we live on the edge of the Far Western Sector with the spaceport just outside the complex. See how long an exterior boundary we have. It's an important sector to maintain."

He moved the cursor to the opposite side of the screen.

"As far as you can get from us is the Far Eastern Sector where some people still live above ground. Many work on glass manufacture. Almost half are fisher people who trawl the Tauan Ocean and provide useful food supplement. Some keep dairy herds and actually cultivate above ground, as you'll see."

Their monitors dissolved to a plough being drawn behind a solar buggy. Birds swooped around the curling clods of earth forming in its wake. Then there were close-ups of buildings nearby covered with cackling starlings jostling for position, two-tone excrement accumulating below. Further shots followed of row upon row of trees weighed down by close-packed, glossy birds. As the class produced sounds of disgust, Tess curled her lip in contempt.

"They're really not as repulsive as you make out," said Ben. "Starlings are our enemies because they're great competitors for food, space and therefore survival. Never forget our Survival Code. Far Western has always been one of the highest placed sectors for prevention of Bird Break-Ins. We need to keep that up. So remember: never go outside, always inform Administration of damaged doors and glass and report immediately if you believe a bird is inside the system. Remember the Survival Code."

Al walked her back to her front door. Well, Fay and Jon's really. As Administrator, Fay had a sizeable apartment which was always warm and dimly lit. Tess had been given the spare room and Fay had found new clothes for her.

"These are so tight. How long were you on that shuttle?" she asked.

Tess shrugged. "A long time."

"Walk through the growing areas with me later?" asked Al at her door.

"No. I'll go for a ride on the buggy."

"Oh, well."

Jon had given her the small vehicle. On non-schooling days he had taken her all over Far Western on his own two-seat scooter and shown her how he inspected the glass canopies and their supports and initiated repairs if it seemed necessary. On one occasion he had decided that the state of the glass was an emergency. After setting off an alarm, klaxons blared all over the section. A suited Break-In squad arrived, some members pounding in on foot, others on individual scooters but the majority on a huge fourteen seat buggy which arrived with orange lights flashing.

Jon's gift was her pride and joy. Thanks to him, she already knew the thoroughfares of Far Western well. After a short time using the buggy she could find her way around better than any native. Few Tauans had need to go out and seldom risked getting lost in the covered corridors and the repeating pattern of T-junctions, crossroads and squares. Tess found that if she wished she could easily avoid the few other road users once out in the agricultural zone. The cultivations were shoulder high, above a complexity of pipes and connections, providing plenty of cover for a girl and a scooter of modest proportions.

That evening, she propelled her buggy through the dim dwelling area, humming happily to herself. Once the brightness of the cultivation could be seen, she engaged the engine couple and scooted harder than ever. In a moment she burst out into the blinding brightness of the agricultural zone. Sun dazzled through the glass. The engine gave a little hum of its own then Tess sang loudly as she felt a thrust in the small of her back as the machine surged forward.

When she first had the buggy she had enjoyed the excitement of calling the Break-In Squad but after a while the novelty palled. Tess would watch from a safe distance but, having found no emergency, the Squaddies soon dispersed. So she began making a little real work for them, smashing glass where it was breakable and undermining supports at the places she could find which were vulnerable.

Not in a destructive mood today, she drove to the upward sloping corridor which ended in the door by which she had first entered the canopy complex. One of her favourite places where she often fed the birds, Tess gazed out at the space station open to the infinite sky. Sometimes she opened the metal door and leapt about outside. Other times, as now, she remained inside admiring the great massing of starlings. Their constant movement produced wonderful shifting patterns which always delighted her. They had invaded the whole area, Tess noticed, even beginning to invade the transparent roofing.

Before she left Tess opened the mesh gate. It was hung to automatically swing shut so she wedged it with some bread stored under her buggy seat.

"Have you been to the Youth Club?" asked Fay when Tess returned to the apartment.

"No, I've been riding. That's much more fun."

"I would have thought the corridors of Far Western were far more tedious."

"It's the club that's tedious. The place is boring, the people are boring and the music is stinking awful."

"What about your new friend Al?"

"Bor-ing."

"If Tess says 'bor-ing' again, I'll probably tear her limb from limb," said Jon.

He and Fay were enjoying a traditional Ansh Eve spread with a group of friends who knew that their close relationship was being jeopardised by Tess's constant presence. Her restlessness, her complaints, even her excessive appetite were becoming insufferable.

"I don't know why you put up with her," said Ed. "It's bad enough when your own kids go through that stage but when it's some little brat not even from your own planet…"

"Where else could she go?" asked Jon.

"Far Eastern Sector sounds like a good idea."

"It must be tough for you," said another guest. "You're both so busy with the Break-Ins."

"I must admit, when I'm tired, Tess's constant whining can really get me down," said Jon. "I'm quite glad she's celebrating Ansh Eve with Al's family."

"And what's Al like?"

"Nice lad. Tallish, good-looking. And boring."

There was a silence while they concentrated on their meal then Ed said, "Fay, you're very quiet tonight. You're not worried about the Ansh tomorrow, are you?"

"No." She sighed. "I suppose I'd better tell you. It's Tess."

"We might have guessed."

"Al came to me three days ago and said he'd followed her after they'd had a tiff. It's happened before apparently. She went through all the same manoeuvres to give him the slip and he used the same technique in response. He let her think she'd succeeded then followed. He's got a more powerful buggy than Tess and seems to be very good at concealing himself under the cultivations."

"So?"

"He saw her unfasten exterior doors, wedge them open with chunks of bread then lay trails of food into the interior."

The others sat upright.

"Then she started smashing the glass."

"Smashing glass! That's impossible," said Jon.

"Not on some of the greenhouse sections and that's where she was."

Ed had sprung up.

"I hope it's fixed."

"Yes, it is. I spoke to Tess next day. She denied everything, said Al had a grudge because she jilted him. But when the squad arrived glass was smashed and doors fixed open just as he'd said."

"Perhaps Al did it out of spite."

Fay shook her head.

"He really loves Tess. Head over heels. It upset him to make a report on her but he's a Tauan born and bred. He was really shaken by the Break-In."

"It really happened?"

"Oh, yes. Only a few birds and the Squad took them out."

"Was that the end of a beautiful friendship?"

"Seems not. She's gone to his family for Ansh Eve, anyway. But I asked Al to continue trailing Tess and so far nothing's happened but he admits that when he followed her before, he found mesh doors open. It's what I'd suspected and never dared believe."

"You think Tess has been doing it all the time?"

"It's got to be. Our record was second to none. It's only plummeted this last year."

"Feeding our bread to the pernicious starlings!" exploded Jon.

"Watch that girl," said Ed. "Put a permanent trail on her. But not Al. If he's so smitten he could cover up for her."

"I don't think he would but I'll find somebody else."

"One thing, at least the Ansh won't be as exciting as last year."

"No," said Jon. "Bor-ing."

Birds rose squawking from every feasible perch and the faded flags and bunting danced in the breeze as if the Ansh was still a celebration. As the autoshut engines died, banks of starlings streamed from the ports to the usual universal groan. Ed strode towards the craft. Jon accompanied him, the intention being that he should help to tip out crates of kippers or any other useful commodities if they could be found, a forlorn hope given the huge size of the vessel and the limited time available. Jon was to maintain intercom silence with only Ed communicating. As usual, he made the most of it.

"Main hatch open," he announced.

"Steps extending."

Then, "Reached the foot of the stairway. About to climb."

The onlookers were exchanging pained glances when a figure appeared in the hatchway. Ed preceded Jon onto the ladder just as a communal gasp reached him and he stopped.

"Come on," he growled. "It's a good joke but I know damn well it can't happen two years running."

He continued to mount the stairway.

"Ed, I'm breaking silence," said Fay. "There's a figure in the hatchway."

"I know, a little kid in stretch jeans and a tight tee-shirt saying, 'I'm a little green monster'."

He kept climbing.

"No! It's no joke. It's somebody in a suit complete with helmet."

He stopped.

"Is it Chaz?"

"No, I don't think so. It's somebody really big and broad. Taller than you."

Ed took a deep breath and said, "Okay" and began to move upward again.

At the top he stopped and said, "Er – who are you?"

The stranger pushed forward a huge gloved hand. Intercom proved to be compatible because everyone heard the newcomer say in a gruff voice, "Edward Lukehurst, your starling expert."

Although taller than average, it was his mountainous backpack which caused the optical illusion of massive build. Beneath the helmet he had a grey crewcut and a brown seamed face with regular features. Tauans always settle for short names so to save confusion with Ed, Lukehurst became generally known as Lou.

Ed and Jon helped him unload several large and heavy sacks which left no time to hunt for kippers or any other commodity. Besides, Lou assured them there was very little on board worth having.

Lou joined the Ansh Day Supper at the Communal Hall and shared the top table position with Fay, Ed and a variety of dignitaries and their families.

"Tau asked for a starling expert forty years ago," said Ed. "How come you've taken so long to get here?"

"It's a long way." Lou grinned then his face grew serious. "On Earth, lack of funding and maladministration have blighted what was once considered a wonderful system. The Government began making wholesale personnel cuts within the Space Shuttle Service. Automation would replace staffing but, of course, the technology was underfunded. A minimal workforce became swamped by a sea of requests from the planets. I'm afraid it's been one long cock-up ever since. The Service isn't what it was. Nor is Earth. Everything is depleted. It seems a batch of starlings were auto-loaded after I boarded. That wasn't supposed to happen and it was a long time before I discovered them."

Despite Lou's depressing description of Earth, the Tauans were all very buoyant. The starling expert had arrived and might solve their problems. They plied him with questions.

"How will I get rid of the starlings? I'm going to feed them contraceptive pellets. I fed some to the on-board starlings but kept the bulk for Tau."

"How did you become a starling expert?"

"I did a study of starling behaviour for the Earth Agricultural Organization. The birds have been perceived as a crop damage problem by a variety of food producers for generations."

"Yet Earth Administration sent nothing but starlings when Tau asked for garden birds," said the Far Eastern Administrator.

"Many people disagreed with the policy including my great uncle who was also an authority on starlings. Though even he conceded that they could be voracious insect feeders. The truth is, there wasn't much variety of wildlife left on Earth but there were plenty of starlings."

"What beats me is how people on Earth managed to catch and dispatch them in such large numbers," said Ed. "If we could trap them like that we wouldn't have a problem."

Lou leaned back in his chair and hooted with laughter.

Ed looked aggrieved.

"I'm sorry," said Lou. "I thought you'd know. It's like the old Generation Ships. Know about them?"

Ed nodded.

"They trap about thirty birds and pop them into the prepared transport. Nature does the rest *en route*. By the time they reach here I'd guess there'd be about thirty thousand depending on the time in space. Starlings were introduced to America from Europe in eighteen ninety, you know. About seventy pairs were released in New York. By nineteen fifty they'd increased to a hundred and twenty million and the birds had spread over the whole continent. But there are far fewer now."

"How did they get rid of them?"

"They tried all sorts. Noise machines seemed to clear them from tall buildings."

"Where did they go?"

Lou shrugged. "Somewhere else, I suppose. But noise would be difficult for you here at ground level and probably drive the population. Anyway, in the States and elsewhere, they just declined in number."

"But why? How?" asked Fay.

"Who knows? Environmental changes probably."

"Did you live on birdseed on the shuttle?" asked Ed, winking at Tess who sat opposite him.

"You knew of the cargo then?"

"Of course."

"At least you don't have to contend with those birds. They're on a never-ending journey by way of Sigma, Kappa or wherever until their dying days."

The diners exchanged puzzled glances.

"I'll have you know that those birds were automatically released into the Tauan skies somewhat ahead of you setting foot on the planet," said Jon.

"Just like every year," added Ed.

Lou seemed stunned.

"Every year? Thousands of starlings released into your atmosphere? No wonder you have a problem. But how can it be?"

"That's what we'd like to know."

"Some computer loop repeating your original request over and over, I suppose, and inexperienced operatives crazy enough to obey its every order and putting everything on auto. And so involved with internecine wars on Earth that they can barely think about the job in hand."

Elbows on table, he rested his head on his hands. When he looked up, he realised that his fellow diners were staring and that he must present a picture of despair. He forced himself to smile.

"Well, I have a harder task than expected but at least I'm here. There's no doubting you need me."

Lou was given a berth in Ed's apartment and a solar buggy. He travelled the length of the exterior spreading treated pellets and watched starlings strut, swagger and walk over each other in their haste to wolf the food. Though he might smile and admire the sturdy speckled young holding their own in the scrum, he was perturbed. The situation looked bad. Birds smothered every possible perching place and encroached upon the canopies. Deposits of droppings were accumulating alarmingly. They weighed down and obscured the glass in places. Collapse and inefficiency were imminent.

From the first, Tess had taken to Lou. He too had arrived on the shuttle and was an outsider. On non-schooling days she followed him everywhere. Tess pursued Lou and Al trailed Tess.

After the first couple of days, Lou beckoned to her and demonstrated what he was doing. She became his unofficial assistant, legally venturing outside to scatter feed and set traps.

"Who's the kid who keeps following us?" he asked her.

"It's only Al. Ignore him."

"Is he sweet on you or me?"

Before long Lou was ready to move on to other Sectors. He packed a buggy with sacks and hoisted a knapsack onto his shoulder and made his farewells.

"We'll miss you," said Ed, "but you'll be glad not to have that little kid following you everywhere, I guess."

"A young girl maturing into a woman, you mean."

"Do I?"

"Tess is very disappointed she's not coming with me."

"You speak to her then?"

"Oh yes. And she's becoming very knowledgeable about starling behaviour."

"Just so long as she doesn't start letting them in again while you're gone."

"She knows the Survival Code now. I've promised her that when I travel to the Far Eastern Sector she can come too."

"And Fay's agreed?"

"Yes."

"Bearing in mind what you said about Tess, the developing woman stuff, are you sure you're not turning into a dirty old man?"

"Old but nothing more. You may think it sad, Ed, but physical relationships don't interest me at all these days."

Next day he left for the northern Sectors, visiting them each in turn. True to his word, he returned to Far Western so that Tess could join him for the long journey east.

During a break, they sat on a hillside enjoying the fresh open air. Behind them acre upon acre of glass dazzled the eye. Ahead was open countryside and the distant glistening sea.

Lou asked Tess how she came to be on a shuttle arriving on Tau.

Tess began a cock and bull story about being placed on the ship by her wicked stepmother on Eta. Lou stopped her in mid-flow.

"I don't believe a word of it. Etans are famous for doing anything to stop people getting off the planet because of their decreasing population. They used to shoot anyone making a run for the ship, which always seemed a contradiction to me."

Tess gave him a sheepish look and confessed that she'd been in all sorts of trouble, trapped in a web of her own lies at home, at school and with boys.

"I knew they shot people but nobody had tried it since space knows when so I took a chance. I'm a fast runner and looked smaller than my age. Nobody was going to shoot a little kid. I ducked under the barriers at the very last moment and ran. People yelled. I zipped up that stairway and dived through the hatch just as it was closing. Escape."

"And don't you miss your family?"

"No. I hoped I'd get to Earth where it's all happening. Instead I landed up on Tau which, apart from the starlings, is the dullest place in the universe."

"Perhaps you will get to Earth one day. It is livelier but not in the way you think."

They continued their journey. At a thick-walled harbour tavern Lou soon came to appreciate a different diet. Tess, however, turned up her nose at smoked fish, saying no more stinking kippers for her. Instead she enjoyed local bisque beef, cheeses, buttercake and occasionally fisherman's pie.

At the ocean's edge they watched clouds of starlings screeching behind little fishing trawlers. When scraps were thrown overboard, they dive-bombed in chattering squadrons. Lou and Tess threw crumbs and pellets into the air. Starlings swooped and caught them while others squealed and wheeled in anticipation.

"The common starling. There's nothing common about it at all. Gulls used to do this on Earth but they're all gone now so *sturnus vulgaris* has filled the niche."

Later, sunbathing on a cliff top, Lou thought it a good opportunity to comply with Fay's request that he should find out just why Tess let starlings into the Sector.

Her reply was as simple and direct as Lou's question. "Boredom."

"This is a peaceful planet with very little crime so I guess that to many the place and the people seem boring."

"They are boring."

"Maybe you're right but it's not ethical to break their rules and their Survival Code. It's not a game, Tess. The threat is real. Because I've studied starlings I admire them, their tenacity and their ability. But their numbers on this planet are phenomenal and increasing all the while. Human survival on Tau is at risk. Just use your eyes. You can see that birds cram every roof, wall, branch and twig. Now the glass is in danger of collapse. I'm a starling expert and I've never seen anything like it."

He scattered pellets and a flock of birds, handsomely blue-black swooped down. Iridescent plumage shimmering, they scurried and gobbled. More and more arrived. One walked into the throng like a drunken sailor with a rapid limping gait causing a ruckus in which birds ran, hopped and jumped over each other in a cross between leapfrog and square dancing.

Tess laughed and shortly afterwards Lou smiled as he heard a bird imitating her high-pitched giggle.

His backpack now sagged, three-quarters empty and he knew that little remained on the buggy.

"Not a lot left for the Southern Sectors. I'll just have to do the best I can."

Next day they parted, Tess returning to Far Western as Lou headed south.

Klaxons sounded and feet thudded along the thoroughfares of Far Western as the Break-In Squad rushed to repel another starling incursion. It was worse than usual. A whole stanchion supporting the canopy sagged sideways. Nets were dropped from surrounding sections to confine the invasion and then individual birds were hunted down and shot.

Lou arrived back, sacks and rucksacks empty, as people were preparing for Ansh Eve. He learnt that Tess was resident in the only prison cell that the Sector possessed and immediately went to see Fay.

He found only Jon at the apartment.

"Fay's at the office but come in. I can see you've heard about Tess."

"Smashing the glass and encouraging starlings is punishable by imprisonment I take it."

"If proved."

"And you have a witness?"

"Yes. Al. But he's in hospital. It's worse than you think, Lou. Al was following Tess and caught her in the act. She picked up a shard of glass and attacked him then walked off. Fortunately, Fay still had somebody else following Al who was bleeding profusely. He managed to staunch the flow of blood to some extent and got him back to the dwelling area. He'll be okay but will always have a scar down his cheek. Sometimes I feel so guilty. I used to take Tess round with me to do assessments. But for me, she would never know the vulnerable parts of the canopies."

After seeing Fay in the Admin Block, Lou was allowed to visit Tess and later saw Al. The next day he called on Fay again.

"I have a proposal. There are no more pellets and the starling population which is already huge is still likely to grow. You must continue trapping but it barely causes a ripple. The next shuttle is due and probably thousands more birds will be added to the present population. Human survival on Tau depends on somebody going to Earth and ensuring that no more birds are sent and re-programming so that pellets are sent instead. Not just sent but every package ejected automatically on landing so that nobody has to climb aboard and risk being whisked off for eternity."

"So you propose to leave on the shuttle?"

"Yes. But that's not all."

"Oh?"

"I'm sixty-five years old, Fay, and wearing quite well but I don't know how long it will take the shuttle to reach Earth. I hope it might be something like one or two years but it could be thirty. In which case, if I were alive I'd be a feeble old man. That wouldn't do. To get the system changed will be a very dangerous job. All manner of charlatans were vying for power when I left Earth. Who knows what state will exist when the ship gets there."

"At worst. I don't think it would be longer."

"But it would make it impossible to do anything once you're there."

"Not if I take others with me. It could be like the old Generation Ships. A goodly number set out and maybe their children or grandchildren would be the ones to arrive. Know any Tauans who'd like to do that?"

Fay shook her head. "No. Not at such short notice." She paused. "If ever."

Lou smiled. "Just as I thought. Tauans are settlers, not pioneers. That's why I propose to take Tess with me. She's a danger to your future here but if she can be instructed on how to adapt the computers on Earth, she could be your saviour."

"She's always letting starlings in. Why should she agree to stop them at source?"

"She would have to get the better of some quite formidable opposition. Tess is an adventurous girl. I think she'd enjoy the challenge and want to succeed."

"And if it became the case of a Generation Ship?"

"Al has agreed to come, too. He, believe it or not, is still in love with Tess. They could be the couple who save your planet."

Flags waved and bunting flapped as the shuttle landed.

Starlings around the perimeter rose and fell before black clouds of newcomers flew from the ship and formed a vast, undulating letter S.

"Damn starlings," muttered Ed.

He remained with the group by the tunnel. Three other figures were walking towards the shuttle, one tall, one small and one intermediate. Once they arrived at the hatchway, Lou lowered his backpack, turned and called, "Good-bye and good luck."

Everyone broke silence and the words were repeated over and over. Lou hustled his young charges inside and instructed them rapidly about lift-off.

Much later when noise and vibration had ceased and the vessel seemed to be floating silently, Lou spoke with Tess.

They had left Al at a port watching Tau reduce to a pinpoint of light.

"What I should have told you…"

He hesitated.

"Yes?"

"Is that space is very boring."

"I know. I've been there. But Earth will be exciting."

"That could be a lifetime away. That's why I hope you'll be making peace with Al very soon. Rather surprisingly, he holds no grudge against you."

"I don't care. I hate him."

"I don't believe you. You were good friends once. I think you lost your temper when you realised he was following you. Didn't you?"

Tess hung her head. "Maybe."

"I know you went to see him in the Hospital Bay."

"I just lashed out and ran off. I didn't realise I'd hurt him so bad." She paused. "You said a lifetime?"

"Could be."

"A lifetime of kippers and birdseed?"

Lou smiled. "If you know how to get access to the crew quarters, there's a bigger variety of food and plenty of it. And the computer access which might help us make it less than a lifetime."

"A year?"

"Probably more than that. That's why you and Al must make your peace. For one thing, you'll be sharing lessons."

"Oh, no!"

"On the computers. Knowledge you'll need when you get to Earth. You and he will have to access the auto-shuttle system. There will be people who won't want you to. It could be a very dangerous game."

"There, I said Earth would be exciting."

"The three of us will have to work as a team to hoodwink the opposition. So when Al comes through that hatch, I want you to apologise to him."

Tess pulled her face into an enormous pout but then said, "All right. I will."

"Good." He stared at her. "Why did you allow starlings under the glass this time, Tess? I'd stressed the possible consequences for the people of Tau so I can't believe it was simply boredom. Are you just wicked?"

"No!"

"Why then?"

"I like starlings. I think it's dreadful to kill them. I love them. I think they're darling starlings."

Lou grunted. "That's all right then. Although I have to control them, I'm fond of starlings, too. The more you study them, the more you admire them."

"Yes!"

He grinned at her. "You know, I think we're all going to get on just fine."

CYCLOPS

I was relaxing in my favourite spot in the bar on Space Station 40 when I first saw Nella Nelby. I was sitting at the end of the great seamless window with a cool drink and a magnificent view of the cosmos when she entered the Travellers' Lounge.

Nella was tall, slim, dark and beautiful. She should have strode to the bar, head erect, careless of the rabble around her. Instead, she sidled in looking worried and glancing nervously over her shoulder. She still drew a few admiring glances for all that.

It was inevitable that such a magnificent creature, once served her drink, should choose to share my table and show me up as short, pudgy, pale and as plain as a pixel.

Having sat, she became no more relaxed. She perched her travel bag on her knee and hugged it to her as if it might grow rotors and hover away. She sipped her drink diffidently and tried to take in the people around her, myself included, without meeting anybody's eye. And I was trying to assess her without too obviously staring and making her the more embarrassed.

Strictly speaking one should never open conversations in Space Station bars but just occasionally I do.

Thinking that she might feel less tense with somebody to talk to, with astounding originality I asked, "Travelling far?"

She jumped slightly and gasped, "Earth."

"It's a fascinating place so I've heard, but isn't it a little primitive?"

"No. I love it. It's beautiful. You've never been there?"

"It's not on my run," I said.

"That's a pity. It's lovely. Still very wild in places."

"You like wild places?"

"Yes."

"You're having a holiday there, I guess."

"No. Work. I love my work too."

"So do I, though it gets rather routine at times."

She must have been well aware of my occupation as I wore a pilot leisure-suit with shoulder insignia. I had nothing else to wear as a matter of fact, because my luggage had inadvertently been rerouted through Sandergate Phi.

"What do you do?" I asked.

"I'm a linguist and translator," she said. "I work in conjunction with the Planetary Archaeological Service."

"So you often visit Earth then?"

"I've been twice before."

"And you must specialise in Earth languages."

"That's right. I'm also a specialist in Vectis, Palladic and Porteran."

I was suitably impressed, and said so. She in turn said that she was impressed by my being a pilot. Female crew probably outnumber male these days but there are not that many women captains.

She introduced herself then, and I told her my name. She had visibly relaxed once she began talking about her work, so I asked her to tell me some more about it.

"At the moment I'm concentrating on Latin and Greek, particularly Ancient Greek."

"I thought all those languages were ancient."

She smiled and said, "Some are more ancient that others. They are excavating a site on – on an island in the Mediterranean. That is the land-locked sea which, if you remember your Earthian studies, was where many civilisations flourished. Our project is to finally prove that Earth was the cradle of humanity."

"I didn't think there was any doubt."

"Certainly it's a very common belief, but it's almost impossible to prove conclusively. Carbon-dating works on Vectis in much the same way as on Earth and that is proved to have a much more recent civilisation than any Earthian culture. As to the rest, nobody can tell. One can only compare their cultures with the various Earth civilisations. Some academics will consider that a particular comparison is irrefutable proof, others that it's fantasy." Her faced became pained. "But now I have the proof in here."

She indicated the bag still perched on her knee.

"In there? I thought you said it was almost impossible to prove."

"Almost. But this isn't proof that Earth was the cradle of humanity."

"I'm sorry, I thought you said it was."

"This is the proof that it wasn't." Her face seemed to collapse in despair. "Professor Beck is furious and has hinted that my sources are spurious."

"Well it rhymes," I said.

She looked puzzled.

"Furious, spurious," I said.

"Oh, I see."

"And are your sources spurious?"

"No. Certainly not." Her hands hovered over the bag. She seemed in two minds about opening it, then pulled a wry face and shrugged. "Look, this is one part of the proof," she said, undoing the bag and bringing out a folder which she handed to me. "It's only a facsimile, of course, but the source is impeccable, believe me."

"You're not revealing your source?"

"Not to a complete stranger, no."

"I can't say I blame you," I said, riffling through the file. "On the other hand, I can't think why you are telling me, a complete stranger, so much about it."

"I suppose it's that I'm choked at Professor Beck's reaction. I've just got to tell somebody and get it off my chest."

The folder contained the print-out of a spaceship logbook. Basically it was the same as the one kept on my trans-planet run, and on any other ship for that matter. But there was something about this one that was different. The typeface looked as if it had been produced by one of the earliest computerised systems, and there were settlement names that were similar to some I knew but not quite the same.

"Is this very old?" I asked.

"The original is about three thousand years old," she replied.

"Standard years?"

"Yes. I cannot date it accurately because Professor Beck is refusing me access to the necessary facilities."

"That man sounds a real abort-system," I said. "He's jealous, I suppose. He was in charge so he wants all the glory."

"He is a she," said Nella, "and there's no glory. I've proved just the opposite of what we hoped to establish."

"The truth will out," I said, and settled to read the evidence.

I scanned the readings, the navigational detail – which seemed quite meaningless to a modern pilot – and the crew rotas. There seemed little of interest to be gleaned from these so I moved swiftly to the Captain's Remarks section.

At first the trip was uneventful and the captain could afford to be mean with words. Most entries read, "All systems functioning normally. All personnel in good health." There was the occasional excitement of, "Emergency Stations Drill, 004 hours."

That was until they encountered the meteoroids and the Emergency Stations became the real thing.

There was ample warning and avoiding action was taken but it was a particularly dense and deep mass. The captain was either exceedingly skilful or incredibly lucky, for the ship managed to zig-zag more than halfway through the vast band before it was hit. A large mass pierced their hull and demolished two of the stern holds. The adjacent holds resealed automatically, preserving oxygen and life.

The other damage was much less spectacular but caused havoc. Small fragments peppered the hull and many penetrated to places where there was no automatic seal operation and the result was death and destruction. All bulkheads have automatic seal these days, I'm glad to say.

As suddenly as the meteoroids came they were gone. The ship remained at Emergency until every alarm had been dealt with and calm was restored.

"Our crew has been decimated in the strictest sense of the word," wrote the Captain. "Four are dead out of a total muster of forty. We committed their bodies to the wide during the first watch. Of the remainder, nine sustained injuries of some kind. Some damage to the computers occurred, but fortunately the navigational functions are intact. There is also damage to steering and engines, added to which, all emergency and repair equipment was lost in the after holds. Our position could have been infinitely worse. As it is, we can make our way, albeit slowly, to the nearest planet, BK3, under auxiliary solar power."

The captain and crew learnt from the computer information bank that BK3 had been superficially explored three or four generations before and was then sparsely populated by primitive tribes of hunters and gatherers. A more advance group was living by an inland sea and inhabiting its many islands. They had developed agriculture and probably trade for there were watercraft and seaport settlements. Their dwellings were strongly built and permanent. There were some fine structures built of stone which appeared to be public buildings. The planet was rich in a variety of minerals which were largely unexploited by the indigenous population.

"But will it provide suitable constituents for us to meld into pliable, unsnappable plasticite for steering guides and a tough enough steelite for the main engine?" the captain fretted in the record.

Once arrived, the ship went into orbit while information about the planet's surface was monitored. They encountered a very basic problem which they were not expecting. The atmosphere was unbreathable. The reports of the earlier expedition had not included this fact. The captain had presumed that the surface was compatible with human life because if it were not it created such practical problems as to merit some small mention.

"The meteoroid damage to the computer could explain this discrepancy," the logbook read. "Although I would expect a hit to delete a whole tape not a part of one, it is possible that an impact removed the information regarding atmosphere on BK3 from the computer store. Alternatively, it could mean that the surface is perfectly healthy and the computers are at present giving a false reading. In the interests of safety, I must ignore this possibility. All personnel are instructed to wear suits and helmets on the surface while readings are adverse."

A scout car was sent to the surface, piloted by the second in command, Polson, who was accompanied by three crew members, Grant, Vectan and Kirilli.

The mothership continued to orbit the plant and its log would have returned to the mundane except that at the end of each day the captain included the following reports from the scout car.

Day 1: We have landed in an area where a large expanse of water swirls against a jagged mainland fringed by promontories and rocky inlets. This sea is dotted with mountainous land masses which made touchdown a delicate business, but we managed a safe and uneventful landing on one of the larger islands. This gives good readings for minerals suitable for steelite.

So far as we can tell, the population is small and well spread, a tribe of herders. We have seen their animals, which have thick curly coats above four spindly legs and give weird guttural calls.

We feel certain that we were not observed when landing and have used the cragginess and a natural cave as part of our camouflage which is as near perfect as I have ever seen. The most orthodox programmer on landfall cover could find nothing to criticise.

So far so good, but the readings for the atmosphere outside remain a high danger level making our task more difficult. We began drilling inside the cave at once and extraction began. Plenty of suitable steelite material but nothing suitable so far for steer-guides.

Day 2: We have seen many more quadrupeds and also had a closer view of their keepers. They have not seen us. The herders seem to be small in stature but undeniably humanoid. It is hard to believe that these are not oxygen-breathing mammals like ourselves, but the readings continue to indicate insufficient oxygen and also a dangerously high radiation level. Outside the scout car we continue to wear suits and helmets. They make the physical effort of mining hot, laborious and slow. We have still found nothing suitable to meld into plasticite for steer-guides and, more worryingly, the readings do not show anything suitable in the vicinity. We would be grateful for the nearest location from the mothership readings to save time when we are ready to move on.

Day 3: Drilling in suits and helmets in a high surface temperature makes for slow, tiring work. All the same, we are making good progress. In two more days we shall have enough steelite and to spare for the main engine.

We are surrounded by grazing animals today and also saw a humanoid much closer; small, slender, thin-limbed and clad in a short tunic.

Captain's eyes only: Code 448321967: I note your confidential remarks about no readings on planet for minerals suitable for plasticite manufacture. When we have finished the steelite mineral extraction in two standard days we shall make a minimum altitude scan to search for low-level plasticite deposits not detectable from orbit height, as instructed.

Day 4: The mouth of the cave is broad and one of the quadrupeds strayed in today. Kirilli jokingly said that she would measure the creature for plasticite readings and turned the gauge on it. To our amazement there was a low reading. Grant and Vectan were astounded when I said to bring the creature aboard for further tests. Kirilli thought it was a huge joke and chased it around the cave. When it looked to escape the way it had come I ran to the opening and frantically waved it back. The others thought I was mad so I felt obliged to explain that there was no record of any minerals suitable for plasticite manufacture detectable from orbit.

The animal was brought into the scout car for analysis. The smell was appalling. The extractors are going full blast. We may have to wear suits and helmets inside the car if this stench does not abate. The plasticite reading was given off by a long, tough, stringy tendon which is part of the interior workings of the creature. To extract sufficient for our purposes will be a laborious, messy, stinking and horrendous task but I shall await your instructions.

Day 5: The humanoids do not appear to be searching

for the missing animal. Their tending of the creatures seems to be extremely haphazard. We caught two more quadrupeds close to the cave mouth and extracted the required part inside the car. I have decided that in future we shall wear suits and helmets and do the work in the cave.

Later we herded six animals into the cave. Although we are improving with practice at our tasks we could not deal with them all at once and rolled boulders across the cave entrance to stop those creatures not being dealt with from wandering off.

Day 6: Two herders were searching for stock today. We, in fact, had several of their creatures in the cave. The animals were making a terrible din with their hoarse calls until stunned, but they remained undiscovered. Grant has manufactured some camouflaged fencing to put across the mouth of the cave.

Vectan suggested that as there seem to be very few herders and they are, in any case, primitive and without weapons, it would be a good idea to set up a whole series of fences outside the cave. If we could manage to herd a hundred or so creatures within this corral we could effect a quicker and more efficient system of extracting the plasticite based on our present routine. This will make our presence very apparent to any observers on the surface and I feel the need to ask permission to put the plan into operation.

Day 7: The scheme is working well. We fenced round about fifty animals today and could have encircled more if extra fencing units had been ready. We saw two small humanoids on the skyline for a brief period.

Day 8: All goes well. More fence units have been erected. We managed to cram the increased area with creatures. Kirilli and I chasing, coaxing and manoeuvring the wayward beasts inside the circle. We must have looked very ridiculous at times in the course of our duties. Whilst we were leaping about like maniacs Grant and Vectan were working steadily. We are incinerating the unwanted remains of the creatures.

Day 9: Vectan reported two small humanoids peering over the fencing today. As soon as he saw them they were off and away over the rough terrain with the speed and dexterity of mountain animals.

I fear that they will report our activities and bring back herders in great numbers, perhaps armed. I have ordered that if the intruders appear again they must be stunned and detained to prevent this but already it may be too late. We need three more standard days to complete our task.

Day 10: No herders have come to interrupt our work nor have the two humanoids who were spying upon us been seen again. The work progresses well.

Day 11: Grant caught one of the spies actually right inside the cave. She stunned the humanoid immediately and tethered it to a fence unit within the cave. Vectan is certain that this is one of the two which he observed on Day 9.

Day 12: We live in fear of massed herders coming to look for their own, but so far nothing has happened. We would like to communicate with this small being now that it is conscious but it is impossible. We cannot remove our helmets outside the scout car and we cannot take the humanoid inside for fear of contamination. We believe that it has not yet reached full stature but that even fully grown would be quite small compared to us. The work goes well and if, by good fortune, we have no interruption will be completed tomorrow.

Day 13: The work is completed. The humanoid was released and driven over the ridge. Kirilli remained on the peak to make sure it did not return to see the scout take off. Grant, Vectan and I cleared the site and so far as possible removed all trace of our temporary occupation.

Kirilli has returned to the scout and we are now about to take off and look forward to docking with the mothership.

There the record ended.

I looked up at Nella, who was sipping her second drink.

"It makes fascinating reading," I said. "But I just don't see what it proves."

"BK3 is the Earth, of course, and if an expedition visited it while the indigenous population were primitive herders then Earth was not the cradle of humanity."

"But there's nothing here to prove that BK3 is the Earth. In fact, it seems unlikely. It has no oxygen and is irradiated."

"It has low oxygen and is irradiated," Nella corrected. "But I suspect that their computer was at fault after the battering they received. I think they probably wore suits and helmets on the surface quite unnecessarily. The fact that the figure three appears in their classification of the planet is interesting, don't you think? Earth, after all, is the third planet out from the sun within its solar system."

"But that's hardly conclusive," I replied. "In essence, there's very little to go on. There's nothing to indicate the name of the ship, its route, its destination or when the journey was made."

"There are place names mentioned there," Nella replied, "though, as you said, the spellings are weird. They could fit in with the ship having to make an emergency landing on Earth but that's just by the way. What really clinches it is the manuscript which ties in with the ship's record or, more properly, with the scout car's reports."

She began to reach into her travel bag, but then thought better of it.

"The original of this, against all the odds, was preserved by a freak of nature on the planet Earth. I can't afford to lose it because I have no other copy. I honestly think Professor Beck would have me killed to get it back. I'm pretty certain I've been followed half across the galaxy anyway."

She looked up and glanced around the bar and then froze, staring with horrified eyes at the main entrance to the bar.

"Oh no," she whispered.

"What is it?" I asked and looked round at the person who had just entered.

The man was vast. He was also the ugliest human I had ever seen. His overall shape was pyramidal, and the top of his triangular head spread out and down to jowly folds of skin around his collar.

"It's Doctor Roskopf, Professor Beck's assistant," gasped Nella. "If only there was some way out of here without him seeing me."

"But there is," I said, pointing my thumb over my shoulder. We decamped through the female urination facility, breathing sighs of relief that there was still sexual segregation in some things. With my knowledge of the Space Station's layout it was a simple matter for me to lead Nella down fire chutes, up emergency stairs, through air-lock cavities and even along cable ducts. Not only was Doctor Roskopf unlikely to know the way but he would also be hampered by his bulk. Even so, once arrived at the twenty-second staging I suggested that Nella kept out of view while I checked that there was nobody about.

We entered my apartment unobserved, and locked ourselves in. After a slight hesitation Nella handed me the document which seemed to be the cause of our tortuous route. The heading read, 'An account from my childhood'.

"I thought you said this was a manuscript. I expected it to be written by hand in the ancient way," I said.

"The original is," said Nella, "but this is my translation from the Greek."

I read:

I, being Aeneas, son of Philippos, and drawing near to the end of my days, wish to set down a true account of certain events during my childhood by which the gods ensured that I should follow the same path as my father while my sister became a wanderer and followed her own fate.

I would also like to set down that my sister Homa and I, though estranged from our youth, were reunited and reconciled before her recent death.

My history begins with the happy times tending the summer flocks with Homa. That is how I would always wish to remember my childhood, ignoring the biting winds of winter and the weariness and forgetting the fear and shame which came later.

Homa was four years my senior and very strong and agile. For all that, my father's flock often spread far and wide while she sat beneath a tree daydreaming.

"Homa," I would say, "please let us round up the strays. Father will be angry and whip us if any are lost."

"You go back if you wish," she would reply, "I'll follow later. After all, they have to spread out and find fresh grazing. They would starve otherwise and then Father would whip us for letting them die of starvation."

Eventually she would realise that she had tarried too long and then would follow long hours retrieving the stock. Homa striding out, suddenly full of energy with me trailing, despondent, small legs tiring.

It was inevitable that accidents would befall our sheep and there were beatings. Homa suffered most. She was the elder child and in charge of me as well as the herd. I must admit I was whipped but once and liked it little. Homa probably had more thrashings than she need for she had a defiant tongue which provoked our father and all our mother's pleading could not save her.

The summer after our mother's death was very hot.

The slightest movement caused cascades of perspiration. Naturally the sensible thing when tending sheep was to sit under a tree. I made no objection.

Often we had provision for several days and nights and we slept under the stars. On one such occasion Homa told me that she had had a strange dream of a monster who roared thunderously and caused a rushing wind. In her dream the monster had swallowed all of our sheep.

The dream affected Homa for we set off early that morning to check on our flock. In fact, we spent the next few days checking. There was no point in rounding them up for this was the time of year when they could roam far and wide to find the best grazing. Despite this, Homa encouraged the furthest of them towards the area where the main body was dispersed. I never expected to exert so much energy in that fierce heat but I accepted it. If all our sheep were swallowed by a monster Homa could expect floggings for the rest of her days.

The dream came true a few days later. We saw a monster near the high peak of the island and I felt the blood drain from my face through fear. Rooted to the spot we watched. It made no awesome noise. It was entirely silent which, in some respects, was more frightening. Although we saw it from a distance we could perceive that it was huge, a giant with great girth and enormous height. It had a grey shiny pelt and the shape of a man. Its movements were slow and clumsy. When it turned its head on our direction we could see that it had a ghastly blank face with one huge dark eye in its centre.

My heart has never beaten so fast as the day I saw that ogre. At first my legs turned to jelly but soon they were recovered enough for me to spring up and run from that place as fast as I could. But it was not to be. Homa grasped the top of my skinny arm with her long bony fingers and pulled me into the parched bracken.

"Keep down, you fool," she hissed, bruising my arm with the tightness of her grip. "Don't let it see us."

So we kept down. Homa told me to stay where I was and wriggled forward like a snake to watch the terrifying creature. I was then convinced that she was the bravest person in the world. She came back to me and said that the giant had disappeared from view behind some rocks. We retreated, keeping close to the ground, to the place where we had slept that night.

"Homa, let's go home and tell Father what we have seen," I said. "We cannot stay here."

"You go home and tell Father what we have seen," she whispered. "I shall stay here and try to look after the sheep. Tell Father to come as soon as he can and to bring his bow and arrows. Otherwise surely this monster will eat the entire flock just as in my dream."

I was happy enough to go home, to get far away from the giant, though I felt guilty about leaving Homa behind on her own. I was frightened also at the prospect of being alone.

"Come too," I said. "I shall be afraid travelling without you."

But she would not come.

"Father will whip me for leaving the sheep," she said. "You go and tell him that we need his help."

So I went alone, feeling safer and happier the nearer I got to home. If I had foreseen my reception I would not have been so glad. My father would not believe my tale. I pleaded with him, I begged him to come and bring his bow. I told him of Homa's dream and how later we had seen the real monster.

He shook me until my teeth rattled.

"What nonsense is this?" he roared. "Has Homa sent you with this rigmarole because she has lost more sheep than ever? Get you back to the grazing and tell Homa that when she returns she will get the biggest thrashing of her life if any of our flock is gone."

"But it's true, Father," I cried. "I saw it with my own eyes. A great tall monster."

I stretched my arms up and out the more to explain its vastness. My father gripped my barely perceptible biceps where Homa had already bruised me, making me shriek.

"Tell me lies would you, boy? Well, I know what the best thing to do with liars is."

That was when I experienced my first and only whipping. It was a turning point in my life. After that I always told people what they wanted to hear and that, I suspect, is why I became a successful and prosperous man. I rarely said what I thought, and seldom did as I said.

Success was in the future and seemed all unlikely then as I dragged my painful body back up the mountain to the summer grazing to deliver the awful news to Homa.

"We are between Scylla and Charybdis," she groaned.

"Between what?" I asked.

"On the one hand is a horrendous ogre," she replied, "on the other Father's wrath and the strength of his arm."

I shuddered.

"There is only one thing to do," said Homa, staring wide-eyed into my tear-stained face. "We must kill the monster and drag it back home. Then Father will believe us."

I was appalled.

"Kill it? How can we kill it?"

"With our knives. Creep up on it when it sleeps. Even monsters must sleep."

I doubted that and said so.

Our knives were small and not very sharp. Mainly we used them to cut bread, cheese and fruit; occasionally to free sheep from briars. Then we would sharpen them sufficiently to saw through the tough tendrils.

Now Homa honed her knife as never before, not only the blade edge but also the end into a sharp point.

"That would kill anybody," she said, "even Cyclops."

"Even what?" said I.

"Cyclops. That's what I call the monster because he has one huge round eye."

Quaking with fear I accompanied my sister back to the area where we had first seen the giant and there we saw it again. It lumbered around, building a stockade. This was made of shiny silver wood but it was not birch and it was not cedar and it was not like any other timber I have ever seen. This fence when built encircled a wide area and also enclosed the mouth of a cave which was the monster's lair.

Imagine our horror when a second giant came out of the cave and began to help the first.

"Two Cyclops," gasped Homa.

Many of our flock were in the vicinity and the two monsters began rounding them up and driving them inside the paling as if it were shearing time. They were slow and lumbering but for all that they managed to pen a score or more sheep. Homa looked on horrified. I looked on terrified.

Then they began to pick out one or two from those that were captured and push them through the opening into the cave.

"What are they doing with our sheep?" asked Homa. "We must find out."

The bravest thing I ever did was to follow Homa, creeping, crawling to the palisade, breath held, my tiny knife grasped in my hand.

We could not see into the cave so we learnt nothing, but we saw the creatures close to. I believed at first that they were blind, for their monstrous single eye seemed to reflect the land and sky and did not appear to focus on anything or have the means of focusing. That explains my carelessness. I tried silently to indicate to Homa that I believed that they could not see but as I gestured my knife slipped from my hand. It clattered against the fencing as it fell and the nearest monster whirled round and began to lurch towards us. Homa and I jumped up and raced away, leaping over rocks and thorn bushes with the speed of fear.

I slept little that night. I racked my brains to think how we might convince Father of the Cyclops' existence without having to kill them. Homa would deem it impossible to kill two of them, I decided, and I was heartily glad. We would not have to put her desperate plan into operation.

But Homa insisted that she could still carry out her plan. She would kill both giants swiftly and silently while they slept. I could see the impossibility of her scheme. The first creature attacked would cry out and awaken the other and she would be caught and probably killed. It needed two, acting in unison, for the plan to succeed but I could not bring myself to volunteer my services. Homa, in any case, made it clear that she did not want me with her as I might drop my knife as before. She would kill the first she said, and if the other awoke she would put out its eye with a sharpened stave before it could grab her.

The stave was whittled and at nightfall Homa crept down to their stockade planning to work her way slowly and carefully to the cave under cover of darkness. Later she would need my help in dragging one of the carcases home to Father, she told me.

So I remained on the hillside alone in the darkness and full of fear. The dawn should have brought relief but it merely added to my anxiety, for Homa had not returned from the giants' lair.

I watched the cave mouth all that long hot day and saw no sign of her. I became convinced that she was eaten by the Cyclops.

If I could have foreseen how petrified I would feel that

second night alone in the dark I would have set off home before dusk. I sat wide-eyed in the pitch black imagining Cyclops creeping up on me and about to pounce.

At the first glimmer of dawn I began to move towards home, slowly at first, making sure that I made no noise, then faster and less quietly, and finally I ran headlong.

My father accompanied me back to that place, tight-lipped, disbelieving, expecting only that many of his sheep had either come to harm or were missing. His expectations were fulfilled. The giants were gone, their sheep pens had disappeared and there was no sign of Homa. I was convinced that she was devoured by the Cyclops but would not say as much to my father knowing that he would not believe me.

Homa reappeared a day or two later. The Cyclops had kept her captive but had not harmed her. They had cooked and consumed scores of sheep and then driven her away to the other side of the island. When she felt enough courage to return every trace of them had disappeared.

My father was contemptuous of Homa's tale of monsters and I, past the turning point, would no longer corroborate her story. She was reviled, beaten and flung across the hearth where she struck her head on a cooking pot. My father never spoke civilly to her again.

The loss of the sheep was a setback to the family fortunes but we seemed to recover well enough. Soon Homa and I were out guarding the flock again.

Homa never lost another sheep. She worked hard and she worked long. She had great physical fortitude. She began to suffer from headaches which sometimes affected her sight but still she would work on.

When my father died, all his goods were bequeathed to me. I would like to record that I did not drive a half-blind woman from my house to fend for herself. Homa chose to go.

It took her longer to assimilate the lesson which I had

learned so young but eventually she did. She began to tell people what they wanted to hear. My sister, as you know, became renowned as a story-teller and much in demand. She is now much more famous than me although I am the richest man for many miles around.

Now I weep with joy that my sister returned home before her death and we were reconciled. I shall always remember her as young, strong and agile as in the happy days when we tended the sheep on the summer pastures.

Nella was staring at me when I looked up. "Now you see, don't you?" she said.

I was still trying to marshal my thoughts and, in my mind, fit in all the pieces of the jigsaw.

"I see the problem," I said, "if these are genuine."

"They are, they are. Professor Beck and Doctor Roskopf would not be going to such trouble if they believed otherwise."

"Yes, what exactly are they up to?" I asked. "I thought these documents were copies, transcriptions."

"Yes. The spaceship journal is a direct copy but the other is my translation. There are not that many people who could do such an accurate translation. They would feel pretty safe if they could destroy that," she said, pointing to the typescript which I held, "and put paid to me."

"Would they really murder to suppress the truth? If there were a lot of money involved I could understand it but most people are not bothered about the past."

"There is money involved, grants, sponsorship, livelihoods, but mainly it is academic reputation and the opinion of future generations."

"You say you're going to Earth, but won't that be very dangerous if they really are so murderous?"

"It would, but I'm afraid that I didn't tell you the truth. I'm running away from Earth. I will return but only when I can reproduce these documents on a massive scale together with my own commentary on their discovery. There will be too many to track down then and therefore little to be gained from liquidating me."

"And where are you running to?"

"Wherever I can reach without them knowing and following. It has to be somewhere sophisticated enough to have facilities to produce copies of my finished work in large numbers."

I was not convinced of the life-and-death nature of the situation but decided to err on the side of caution where possible deaths were concerned.

"I can offer you a place on my ship to Sandergate Theta," I said, "but I would have to check your papers."

"You would be welcome to check them but I cannot risk my name appearing on a flight list or going through the normal embarkation procedures. I'm sure that every flight is being searched."

"That's why I would have to check your papers. Your name would not appear on any list and you would bypass all the normal procedures. You would be my personal guest and share the privacy of my quarters unseen by any other passenger, if necessary."

Her face lit up with a wonderful smile and she produced her papers for me to examine.

"The truth is," I said, "I would be unable to get you an ordinary flight for we are fully booked. With the rare mineral finds on Theta it's becoming a very popular place just lately. Everyone is rushing in hoping to make a fortune."

One or two irritating habits apart, Nella was an excellent travelling companion. She was cheerful and helpful and during my off-duty spells adapted her mood to mine. She would make conversation when I needed chatter and could keep silent without seeming oppressive when

I needed peace. There was plenty of time for me to pick holes in her thesis and plenty of time for Nella to refute them.

I helped her to disembark discreetly at Sandergate Theta long after the other passengers had left. I have never seen her since.

Sometimes I wonder if it was just an elaborate plan to get a quick and free passage to Theta. Certainly many people were desperate to get there at that time, though the boom is over now. Yet those documents would have been hard work to forge and seemed so genuine. I feel better in myself for recording the whole affair just in case there is something in it. Naturally, the episode has made me ponder the origins of the human race.

One should never open conversations in Space Station bars but just occasionally I do. When you have seen every video and played every computer game and all other entertainments have palled, conversation can seem a blessing.

Certainly it can be an improvement on staring into space.

MEETING THE QUOTA

On our second day in Felston, a gloomy steel town, the whole population gathered in colourful costumes and carnival atmosphere to see a woman named Melinda hanged in the public square.

She stepped, smiling, to the edge of the platform, raising both arms in triumph. A roar of approval rose from the crowd followed by singing and happy chanting. Amid drum rolls and incessant cheering she moved to the noose and the folds of her long white robes were swirled about her feet.

Wearing a black mask and a harlequin costume revealing the shape of a woman, the hangman stepped up and fitted the rope around Melinda's neck.

Pipes and mandolins added to the din so that, when the trap was sprung, I only imagined the sound of the sickening jolt and snap.

Still playing, the musicians moved up onto the dais and obscured from view the cutting down of the body. After a pause, heavy brocade curtains surrounding the base of the platform parted in the middle, two tabarded trumpeters pulling them to right and left. They sounded a fanfare and a gilt catafalque with a scrolled lid emerged on large, intricately carved wheels. Men, women and children in fancy dress moved forward to haul on beribboned ropes.

The cortège moved slowly through the cheering throng in the square, left by way of a narrow street, also seething with people, and entered a building with the words MEMORIAL PALACE sculpted within the pediment of its classical frontage. Grating double doors closed behind the ornate coffin.

Boscombe exhaled a noisy breath down the back of my neck. "So that's how their Quota System works."

"Stunning," muttered Harry. "I wonder if Anton Lambert saw one of these ceremonies before he disappeared."

In the Ploughshare, a solid mass of people stood between us and the bar. The noise was deafening. Everyone shouted to make themselves heard above everyone else.

Kathy, the barmaid, saw us and sang out, "Make way for the Peacekeepers!"

Drably dressed till now, today she wore a garish chequered dress and sported a boater tipped to a saucy angle. A miniature gibbet attached by a spring to its centre bobbed with her every move. People clamoured round and perspiration streamed down her flushed cheeks as she plied the pumps.

"What'll it be? Alc or Non?"

"Alc."

Unlike the mob, we'd drunk Non-alcoholic all day.

"That's it. Getting in the swing now. Be a bit quieter for you over there."

The gallows on her hat bounced as she nodded towards an empty cubicle on the end of a groaning row. We fought our way over.

The other alcoves were crammed with more people than the dingy wooden benches and tables were intended, all singing, cheering, calling out toasts and slogans in a deafening cacophony. Our booth had a scribbled notice, "Residents Only", tacked on the table end.

Boscombe squirmed in beside me and pressed up as close as he could.

"Hey, it's not that cramped, Boscombe."

"Max, please!"

Harry Granville, our boss, sat opposite. He and I usually worked as a pair, often sharing a bed as well as ideas and a general rapport. Having three people on the investigation put paid to that, for Harry would never risk discord, so Max Boscombe's presence didn't exactly delight me.

In fact, there was a fourth member of the team, Sarah Loveridge. As our scientist, she had different priorities and had remained at Coriander.

Harry slid his leg against mine under the table and kept it there.

"What do you make of it, Gless?"

"Decidedly odd."

"How the hell do they brainwash them into doing it?" asked Boscombe.

"Good question, Max. This?"

Harry raised the beaker of cloudy liquid in his hand.

Boscombe pulled a face. "Disgusting stuff. My mother made a much smoother drink with potato peelings so hell only knows what's in this."

"Come on," I said, always willing to argue the toss with him, "their resources are limited and it's not too bad after the first mouthful."

"Are resources so limited that people would volunteer to be hanged for the sake of booze for everyone else and a lot of razzamatazz?"

"Nobody's that altruistic," I said. "Oh-oh. Here comes the mayor. Wondering how we gave him the slip, no doubt."

Mayor Johnson, with a face like thunder, began to push his way to the bar. Kathy saw him and tipped her gibbet in our direction.

The sudden change from angry glower to accommodating beam was breath-taking.

"My dear guests, my apologies," Johnson gabbled as he approached. "We got separated. I do hope you managed to see the ceremony and everything was to your satisfaction."

"Yes, we had an excellent view," said Harry, pointing to the seat beside him.

The mayor flopped down.

"Did Captain Lambert see the ceremony before he disappeared?"

"No."

"So he didn't know that people volunteered."

"It may have been mentioned. The Carnival ceremonies often encourage others to volunteer later."

"But Lambert wasn't told?"

"I don't think so. It wasn't a Carnival Day. They're seasonal, four a year. We presumed that he knew that the Carnival Ceremony was part of the Quota System. After all, he'd come as a result of an earlier report by the two scientific investigators from Centrum who researched into why our system is so successful."

"But Kepler and Irving don't mention Carnival."

"Are you sure?"

"Positive. I've read the reports about sixty times. Maybe you presumed too much. Anyway, you didn't mention Carnival hangings to Lambert?"

"No. He visited the town and saw the steelworks, the same sort of tour which you'll have tomorrow. He was just shown round the works and Home Farm then stayed here at the Ploughshare for another night before leaving."

"For the sector capital?"

"Yes. For the Chancellery at Coriander. They had other visits lined up for him: quarries, factories, you know the sort of thing. I'm sure you'll be doing much the same. He stopped at Largo, so I'm told, which is on the route and decided to go searching in the area and then disappeared."

"Searching for what?" asked Harry.

The mayor shrugged.

"Let's hope we don't disappear," I said, opening my eyes wide in pseudo-innocence.

"My dear Captain Gless, let me assure you…"

"Essenden," interrupted Boscombe. "Captain Gloria Essenden, known as Gless to her intimate friends. Aren't you, Gless?"

"And a few hangers-on and a host of would-be intimates. Is it always women at the Carnival, Mayor Johnson?"

"Women?"

"On the scaffold. Today both Melinda and the hangman were women."

"Ah! No, Captain… Essenden."

"Call me Gless. Everyone does," I said, darting a glance at Boscombe.

"It varies. Sometimes all male, sometimes mixed: a female officiant and male recipient or vice versa."

"Just the luck of the draw, eh?" said Harry.

"And is it always one, er, recipient or sometimes more?"

"Only one. Now, please excuse me. I'm so glad to have found you well but Carnival's always a demanding day. We look forward to seeing you at the Residence tomorrow morning, Colonel, for your final tour."

"Fine. We'll be there."

Johnson struggled back through the bellowing crowd as Boscombe hugged me. "We won't let you disappear, Gless. You can rely on me to look after you."

I wriggled irritably.

"Take your hands off the woman, Max," said Harry, placing his other leg the further side of mine and squeezing, "you're on duty. Are these people on the level, Gless?"

"No. It's just like Coriander. They're charming and helpful on the surface but underneath they're on tenterhooks."

"Mm. Hiding something. Maybe we shouldn't have left Sarah on her own. Splitting two and two might be better in future." He squeezed my leg a little harder. "Still, I don't think we'll disappear. There'd be too much of a stink and more investigators trampling everywhere. They'll try and bamboozle us." He grinned. "No chance."

That night, somebody tried my bedroom door. Not Harry. Probably Boscombe feeling lucky. Whoever, it didn't alarm me. Peacekeepers are trained to look after themselves. I slept.

"Please follow me," said the messenger boy at the mayor's Residence.

I lagged behind on the staircase studying dark, monochrome portraits of former, well-fed mayors.

We were led along a first-floor corridor overlooking an inner courtyard. Wicker skips waited to be loaded onto a large transport, while the driver held open doors for his passengers. I recognised a trumpeter from the ceremony.

A woman hurried out from a door below as the musician looked up and saw me. Seeing his glance, she slowed and turned. In that instant our eyes met. Abruptly, Melinda turned her head away and hastened around the vehicle.

I caught up with Harry and whispered in his ear.

He twitched an eyebrow at me. "Sure?"

"Certain."

"Any chance of viewing Melinda's body in the Memorial Palace?" he asked the mayor. "Before we go on our tour?"

"That would be impossible. The body has already been cremated."

"I think we'll take a look at the building, anyway."

"Very well," said Johnson, gloomily. "I'll get the key."

The building's interior proved to be a crematorium with flimsy wooden coffins stacked against one wall. A trolley system hauled the bodies into the consuming fire but the furnace felt surprisingly cold.

"Are the bereaved family given the ashes?"

"No. They get a plaque on the wall. The ashes are scattered in the hills."

We strolled round looking at the tiny shield-shaped memorials on the walls.

"No dates," I said.

"These are the most recent," said Johnson.

"Where's Melinda's plaque?" asked Harry as we left.

"I'm afraid it hasn't been inscribed yet."

The steelworks stood eerily silent as we entered. Resources were such that the furnaces could be fired only three days a week. The workforce laboured a further three days on the land. The seventh was a rest day.

Home Farm, our next port of call, had none of the cosiness the name implied. Rows of huge steel storage barns were surrounded by vast growing areas stretching towards the distant hills. Silence also reigned here.

"Where are the workers?" asked Harry.

"They're on holiday."

"I thought yesterday was rest day."

"Yes but also Carnival. They get an extra day off."

Harry nodded. "Makes sense. There must have been a few sore heads this morning."

Before we returned to the Ploughshare, the mayor shook hands.

"Our transport will pick you up in the morning and take you to High Col Staging Post for the midday exchange. Coriander requests that one of you practises driving our type of vehicles, both solar and battery."

"Why's that?"

"Resources, I suppose. If you do your own driving while in the Sector, it releases a member of the workforce."

The solar minibus took all morning to grind up to High Col Pass. Once there, it came to a halt with a hiss at the road block in front of the Staging Post. We got off and stretched, surveying the stone and timber building with its steep-pitched roofs intended to shrug off winter snow. The driver hitched the vehicle to one of the booster terminals running along the barrier as another six-seater from Coriander arrived on the other side.

"That's your transport to take you on," said our driver, "and that's my passengers for the run back."

"Why does everything stop here?" asked Harry.

"We're told it's to do with keeping track of resources," he said. "It also keeps us all in our place, but don't tell anyone I said so."

Three passengers emerged from the vehicle on the Coriander side. The two men and a woman, all in black serge uniforms without insignia, climbed, grim-faced, into the bus we had just vacated, their combined bulk making it sink on its springs.

"Who are the heavies?" Harry asked our new driver.

She shook her head. "Factory Inspectors, according to my docket from Coriander Chancellery but it looks like somebody's going to be arrested to me. Right, who's for driving instruction on the return journey?"

"You, I think, Boscombe," said Harry, "while Gless and I sit in cosy togetherness in the back."

Boscombe scowled at first then smiled charmingly at his attractive blonde tutor and soon after said, "Piece of cake! Not much different to a Centrum buggy."

I'd love to carp about Boscombe's driving but he proved very efficient.

After time spent in that dismal, dead-and-alive hole, Felston, I wouldn't have minded going out to booze and boogie. But Coriander wasn't like that. Though wealthier and more salubrious than Felston, particularly in the area around the Chancellery, everything in the busy commercial area came to a halt at dusk. It had none of the night life of Centrum but, then, I suppose nowhere else has.

Instead, we had to sit, formally dressed at a table with Chancellor Frankon, a man whose pencil-line moustache and forced charm caused me grave doubt.

Dinner was a lack-lustre affair. The dining room adjoined the Chancellery's administrative area and sounds of footsteps and doors opening and closing echoed along half-lit corridors. The occasional clatter of cutlery in the high-ceilinged room as the silent waiters came and went, added to the air of desolation.

For once, even Frankon failed to make efforts to scintillate.

"More wine, please, waiter," he called. "Everybody seems tired and depressed after the rigours of the day."

"Not me," said Sarah, who had been pleased to see us back. "I've had a fascinating day with Professor Hudson. That man is brilliant. He should be working for the whole planet not just a sector. Aren't you worried we'll poach him from you, Chancellor?"

Frankon smiled. "Not really. You're getting all the information you could possibly need to replicate his work."

Sarah's face clouded. "Yes… but we still haven't found the missing link."

"The what?" asked Boscombe.

"Well, that's what I call it. The lifestyle as described in

Irving and Kepler's original reports have been tried out in Sector F, but what proves to be successful here in C doesn't seem to work elsewhere. In fact, the experiment verged on the disastrous. I'm trying to find out, with the professor's help, what important facet we may have missed."

"And having seen the Quota System at work in Felston, I've many more questions," said Harry. "Are there Carnivals in every town and are they like the Summer Carnival we saw there?"

"Yes. Every sizeable town in C Sector has a quarterly Carnival and they're all much the same, apart from the weather and seasonal food."

"A Carnival four times a year seems to imply that very few people need to be culled. Not enough to be statistically significant."

"Statistics are, perhaps, part of the explanation for the success of Voluntary Human Culling. Once population is stable, very little adjustment is necessary."

"Or perhaps zoomorphic spongiform encephalopathy is what keeps it down," suggested Boscombe.

The Chancellor turned angrily. "How could that be? There's no animal husbandry in C Sector. Coriander complies with the law and would never subject the planet to those old lethal risks. What would we gain? We'd be risking our lives, too."

"You'll have to forgive Captain Boscombe," said Harry. "That's how the Peacekeepers work, bouncing differing ideas off each other until, hopefully, the truth comes to light. Max favours the theory that there are enormous flocks of disease-ridden animals hidden in deep valleys. Let's face it, the wild terrain would allow for such a scenario."

"I can only reiterate, Colonel, there are no hidden herds, no mad animal disease, no dangerously tainted products. Perhaps Captain Lambert had a similar idea and is lost in the vast wildernesses surrounding Largo as a result. Though, insofar as resources allowed, we mounted a huge search operation."

"The trail seemed pretty cold in Largo but somebody may go back there in a day or two."

"You have carte blanche to go anywhere, see anything. We're proud of our Quota System. It works. Why it didn't work in Sector F, I've no idea."

"Didn't work? It was sheer bloody mayhem. You're going to have to tell us how the system operates socially. That's where the problem lay in F."

"Maybe education is the key," said Frankon. "As elsewhere, our schools dine in the scarcity of resources and the importance of keeping the total number of mouths to feed at the optimum."

"Yet many other sectors are trying to build up their depleted populations," I said. "Feeding everybody from the land requires a big strong healthy workforce."

"Who eat most of what they produce," smiled the Chancellor. "This is what I mean by the optimum. One must have the balance right. Fortunately for us, Professor Hudson has everything worked out. We also do well thanks to his food processing plant which Captain Loveridge saw yesterday."

"Does it make that much difference, Sarah?" asked Harry.

"Yes, I think it does. Soya beans provide high protein but all sorts of other dross that would normally be discarded can be left in, often exceeding the soya content by a huge percentage. The whole synthetic mixture can be flavoured, tarted up and extruded as cutlets, burgers, whatever."

"That sounds absolutely disgusting," said Boscombe.

"You said you enjoyed the first course, Captain," laughed Frankon. "Guess what you were eating?"

"That? Extruded…whatever? That's, that's…"

"Let's get back to statistics," said Harry. "Each community must remain within its population maximum, isn't that so?"

"Quite right."

"Could it be said that the quarterly Carnivals are just show to tempt people into sacrifice? Don't most communities have to cut their population by more than four a year and need encouragement?"

"Some do, just occasionally. Where other days are necessary, outside Carnival, they're less showy. But we like the idea of bread and circuses. People have to work hard for their livings. They deserve a few festivals."

"And if people refuse to volunteer when culling is needful?"

"It's rare but if it happens, the law must be invoked. Administrative officers are sent from Coriander to detain the appropriate people, usually a choice between the excessively old or the illegally new-born."

"What if communities hid their loved ones and reported them culled when they're not? Though I guess if they were successful you wouldn't know about it."

"That couldn't happen, Colonel. People are brought up to respect the law. They wouldn't condone another family trying to hide extra mouths to feed when their own was doing the decent thing."

"You mean they'd rat on them?" said Boscombe.

The Chancellor stared at him malignantly.

Give Boscombe his due, he could get under Frankon's smooth veneer.

Professor Hudson leaned on his desk talking rapidly. He combined schoolboy enthusiasm with thinning hair, a lined face and wispy beard.

"The ingredients are combined under intense heat and acquire high tensile strength during cooling. Before solidification, extrusion is possible into rods of any size, moulds of any shape. As with food processing, material normally rejected as useless can be incorporated. We can even include a percentage of human waste."

"Repulsive," muttered Boscombe.

"I assure you, the product is purified during fusion. If you notice an unpleasant smell as we walk through the plant, that's due only to the chemicals used. Captain Loveridge has details of every formula and specification."

The stench in the factory was sickening.

"How do people work in this stink?" I asked.

"They don't notice after a while."

Walls have ears so we stood in a stiff breeze on the deserted terrace of the Chancellery overlooking the river.

"So let's get this straight," said Harry. "They pretend that somebody has volunteered to hang so that the body's parts can be utilised to boost resources. But it's just show to encourage people to volunteer. The person at the Ceremony doesn't die. So how does the human cull really work?"

"It can't be good," I said. "It's open to appalling abuse."

"I agree and that's probably what Anton found out. Let's see what more we can discover."

Harry decided to visit plastics and chemical plants, quarries and mines in Captain Lambert's footsteps with Sarah in tow querying facts and figures.

"I've got a prize selection of awkward questions here," said Harry, tapping his folder, "and Sarah needs someone riding shotgun. Agreed?"

Splitting two and two hadn't worked out in my favour. Hiding my disappointment, I resigned myself to Boscombe's company on a brief return to Felston followed by a trip to Largo to make further enquiries and comb the surrounding hills.

Driving straight to the mayor's Residence in Felston avoided giving advance warning.

"Although you're Peacekeepers I'll have to get permission from somebody in authority," said the receptionist. "Oh, here's the mayor."

We turned to find not Mayor Johnson but a woman of about thirty hurrying towards us.

"Any problem?"

"The Peacekeepers have come back and want to inspect the Memorial Palace."

"I've no objection. Allow me to introduce myself. Mayor Norris. You must have met Mayor Johnson before."

"Yes. Only three days ago. Where is he?"

"His period of office came to an end. My appointment was made only yesterday so I'm still feeling my way but you're very welcome to visit the Memorial Palace."

We took samples of the ash in the furnace as Harry had instructed and checked the plaques. One to Melinda had been added to the row.

While Boscombe returned the key, I went and booked us in at the Ploughshare and stopped in the bar for a much needed drink.

"So you're back," said Kathy, now dressed in her usual drab. "Just like Anton."

"Captain Lambert came back?"

"Yes."

"The mayor said he didn't. Mayor Johnson."

"He would."

"Also Johnson never mentioned that his term of office was about to end."

"Don't suppose he knew. Rumour has it he wasn't as careful as he might've been. Let you lot see something you weren't supposed to."

"What sort of something?"

"Don't know but I heard the Carnival People reported him."

"So where is he now?"

"Gone to Coriander to be hanged, I suppose."

"Volunteered for the Quota?"

"Been volunteered more like."

"Is that how the Quota System works? People get no choice if they've transgressed in some way?"

She shrugged. "Could be."

Boscombe arrived.

"Kathy says Mayor Johnson was deposed and will probably hang. They'll say it's voluntary. She also says that Anton Lambert came back here."

"What for?"

"Said he'd come back to check population numbers," said Kathy, "diet, lifestyle of a typical town and so on but Anton really come to see me."

"You!" said Boscombe.

Please alienate our witness, I thought. All the same, I looked at her with new eyes. Dark curly hair framed a heart-shaped face, translucently pale without the pressures of Carnival. Besides, Anton had a reputation as a ladies' man.

"Why didn't you tell Captain Boscombe this when he interviewed you last week?"

"Mayor said it'd be more'n my life's worth and I believed him. But I'm crazy about Anton so the middle of the night I come and tried your bedroom door but it was locked."

"You could have knocked or called out."

"Too dangerous."

"And why are you telling us now?"

"Mayor Johnson's gone. I'll take the chance for Anton's sake."

"Good. So what happened when Captain Lambert came back?"

"He went to the mayor's Residence and checked population figures and stuff."

"So Johnson knew Anton came back."

"Of course. Then he visited the factory, the farm and looked into all the production figures. In between times Anton took off looking for herds in the solar buggy he'd been lent by Coriander and kept asking me about animals being kept in remote valleys but I'd never heard of anything like that."

"Ah, well, you wouldn't, would you?" said Boscombe.

"That's what Anton said."

"So he went out looking for diseased cattle and sheep and mysteriously disappeared?" Boscombe asked.

"No."

"What then?"

"Everyone was preparing for the Spring Carnival and he took a real interest, wandering round the streets seeing the hangman signs go up, the decorations, the scaffold in the square. The place has a real buzz then. When the Carnival People arrived he spent a lot of time with them until Mayor Johnson told him they were complaining they couldn't get on with the job. Carnival Day, Anton went off to see the ceremony and I never saw him again."

"Did you look for him?"

"No. You know how busy it gets in here. When the Carnival was over and everyone realised he'd gone, people came from Coriander to search up in the hills. They found the bug, that's all."

"So what they told us about Largo was a complete fabrication."

"Then, at the next Carnival a woman in costume spoke to me at the bar. She'd got a message from him but needed to see me in private. So I told her to come round the back and put her in the cellar until I'd finished."

"And?"

"She was a dissident."

"Dissident? That's the first we've heard of dissidents."

"They're not supposed to exist, an old wives' tale, but they do. She told me Anton crept into the Memorial Palace to spy on the Carnival People after the hanging and they caught him, beat him up. He played dead or unconscious and they nailed him up in one of the coffins. His leg got fractured below the knee but he managed to kneel up, prise off the coffin lid with his back, haul himself to his buggy and drive out of town. But the cell ran down. At dawn, an armed party went out looking for him. Dragging himself about up in the hills, the dissidents saw him and decided any enemy of the administration was a friend of theirs. They rescued him."

"How?"

"Whisked him away to wherever they hang out."

"Where's that?"

"Dunno but the woman started to tell me. Anton wanted me to stay here as their contact. But if things got hot I'd have to get out of town – unseen – and head along the Coriander road as far as the first river bridge."

"And?"

"That's all. We heard somebody coming and she'd already got the hatch undone where the barrels are rolled down. 'Shut this behind me,' she said, then disappeared fast. The manager, who usually keeps out the way if there's any work, come down with two administrators from the Residence. 'What you doing down here, Kathy?' he asked. 'I'm clearing up the God-awful mess the Carnival always makes and me with only one pair of hands,' I said.

'Somebody reported dissidents hiding down here,' he said. 'Dissidents?' I answered. 'There's no such thing'."

We stared up the glove-shaped valley spreading ahead of us. The splayed fingers narrowed to the horizon while the thumb disappeared round a tall outcrop of rock.

"This is another cul-de-sac."

We'd driven to the first bridge and cast about for a while before deciding to follow the river upstream. Dissidents lived in hills and mountains, we decided. While it could manage the gradients, we persevered with the buggy.

"Let's look round the corner."

A third of the way up the next slope the little bug began slithering and sliding backwards.

"Damn. Have to walk now."

Behind the stout column of rock stretched another valley, the mirror image of the one behind us. Boscombe groaned.

"This is useless, Gless. I'll shin up here for a recce."

He uttered a sound and within seconds thudded back beside me.

"We're being followed."

"Damn. We should've been more careful. Kathy said we might be tailed."

"It's not just one, it's a whole gang. Let's quicken up."

With his long legs, Boscombe was a fast mover and I had a hard time keeping up until he stopped to swarm up another tall rock.

"They're lagging behind, just about to discover our bug. Come on, rest and recreation's over. Got to reach the next valley before they get here."

"You reckon they're out to get us?"

"They were out to get Anton so I'm not stopping to ask."

Slipping and sliding, I gasped up the steep slope, Boscombe muttering, "hurry, hurry, hurry." At the top he hauled me over the ridge and we lay watching as the vanguard of our pursuers began to spill into the valley we'd just left.

Skipping and slithering down the new slope, a landslide of stones overtook us. Boscombe stopped short and pushed out a barring arm.

"Who's that?"

The distant figure wore our own sage green uniform jacket several sizes too large.

"A female. Not a Peacekeeper."

She waved, beckoned and made a fast, circular motion with her fists.

We looked at each other, shrugged and ran.

Without us ever catching up, the girl led the way into another cul-de-sac valley and disappeared behind a rockfall at its far end. Beyond the ankle-twisting boulders, trails of thorn and bramble grew. She waited, holding back a swathe.

A dark corridor of rock sloped down towards a pale flickering light. We descended into a wide, flat area lit by the flames of a wood fire. For all that, the cave felt cold and dank.

Several people huddled round the blaze. Others appeared as dark mounds sleeping under blankets beside walls supported by wooden struts. I didn't recognise the bearded man seated on the floor with coverings draped over his legs but Boscombe did.

"Have you obtained permission to grow a beard, Captain Lambert?" he asked.

The girl flopped down beside Anton and he put one arm about her and extended the other towards us.

"Boscombe, isn't it? And Essenden. Excuse me not rising. My leg's playing up today."

I clasped his hand then knelt and turned out my emergency medical pouch.

"Thanks. Leave that with me. I want you both to go with Oona. We have something to show you."

"Oona, eh?" grinned Boscombe. "So that's why the delectable Kathy can't join you."

She scowled and somebody under a blanket tittered.

"Was this a mine?" I asked.

"Yes. Long ago. Silver and lead. All gone now. There are workings throughout these mountains."

"Oona speaks!" cried Boscombe.

"When I need to," she muttered, pulling a brand from the fire. "You have solar torches?"

We nodded.

"Don't use them till I say. Follow my flame."

She headed for an opening at the far end of the chamber, a massive wooden crossbeam supported by two young tree trunks, and set off at her usual cracking pace. We stumbled after, shadows expanding and engulfing our passage along the descending black corridor. In theory, a super fit Peacekeeper, after half an hour I felt desperate for a rest but pigheadedness wouldn't allow me to ask for one.

Eventually, the workings opened onto a gleam of dark water. Oona called a halt and whispered, "We need one torch ready. Hold hands."

She edged to the black pool with us in tow and plunged the brand in. After an explosion of reflected light came total darkness.

"Torch, please."

Boscombe obliged. The white pencil of illumination transferred from his hand to hers.

For a further half-hour we followed this will o' the wisp light until Oona stopped.

"There's a really awful smell," whispered Boscombe. "Is it gas?"

"No. I'm going to put the torch out. Don't move."

At first there seemed utter blackness but soon I realised that a faint light glimmered up ahead.

"Ready?"

The roof became so low we had to crawl. The stomach-churning stench got worse.

When Oona indicated a halt, I could see that the tunnel ended as a small window of light. She squirmed up, looked cautiously over then beckoned to us.

The gap gave a view of part of a pulley system ascending diagonally with sturdy hooks attached.

Boscombe had his handkerchief over his mouth.

"It's a slaughterhouse, isn't it? We haven't found the flocks. We've found the meat."

The empty hooks had passed. Instead, an impaled carcase descended.

"Pork," said Boscombe. "No wonder it stinks."

"Not pork, long pig," said Oona.

I stared in horror as carcase after human carcase passed by, flesh of grey merging to greenish white in the dim light and giving off the overpowering smell.

"Resources," said Oona, inclining her head that we should leave.

Down below somebody began whistling. I slithered back fast, away from the reek of death, hoping not to hear the sound of a cleaver.

"One of you stays," said Anton. "Providing the other one gets back safely, that'll be our guarantee that somebody does something."

"Then it'll have to be Gless to stay," said Boscombe with supreme gallantry. "I'll run the risk of getting back. I don't think Harry would be too pleased if Gless got caught but he wouldn't be too bothered about me."

"Right. Gless stays. Strip off, Boscombe."

"What?"

"You heard. We need all your emergency supplies. And your undies. The winter's going to be damn cold and I don't see anybody getting back before spring."

Thus it was that Boscombe shivered in a biting wind above Felston. Oona, now more talkative, repeated the story that he must stick by for his own safety.

"You know nothing of dissidents, right? You and Gless were up in the hills looking for flocks. You split up, one each side of a valley, and when you looked round she was gone. Not worried at first, then started searching, calling. No, you didn't see any search party, you only wish you had, etcetera, etcetera. Okay?"

"Right."

His teeth were chattering. I hugged him and said, "Good luck, Max."

That's when this account began. First my report book got filled up, then any little scraps of paper anyone could spare. Not many. Resources. You know. Eventually, I wrote on the walls and maybe, sometime, all the scrappy jigsaw pieces will come together.

As a dissident, I learnt to hate the cold and began to appreciate quite meagre luxuries previously taken for granted. In winter we stole from Home Farm but with subtlety. If anybody suspected that supplies were being taken, then guards and ambushes might have been set. The thought of returning to civilisation before long kept me going. Even Felston seems a Mecca compared to the privations of living rough.

Max Boscombe returned in early summer with a pack on his back and looking disgustingly overweight.

"I've come back for good," he said.

"What do you mean?" asked Anton. "Where's the fucking cavalry?"

"They're not coming."

"They didn't believe your story? You couldn't convince them what was happening?" asked Oona.

"Oh, I convinced them. There were all sorts of meetings, discussion groups, advisory bodies. Then the Supreme Council debated the matter and made its decision. The Quota System operated in C Sector made sense in the prevailing conditions, used all available resources economically and ensured that such resources were dispensed in an equitable and just manner, to quote."

"Equitable?" shrieked Oona. "Just? It's an open invitation for the strong to oppress the weak, to make away with all opposition by manipulation."

"Just to prove I'm here to stay…" Max began to strip, strewing several sets of underclothing around his feet.

"Hey!" said Anton. "That's great."

"It'd be even better if we were going back to warmth and real food and drink."

"If you decide to go back to the Quota System, Gless, I'll come too. Leave all this stuff for whoever wants to stay."

"Right! Let's work out how to get across C Sector without being caught and extruded, then live happily ever after in the civilised world of Centrum."

"No, you haven't cottoned on. The Supreme Council not only approved the Quota System for C Sector but also decreed that such a logical way of utilising limited resources should apply to manufacture throughout the planet. The legislation is still being worked through to ensure that there's no risk of transmission of disease but, pretty soon, Quotas are going to operate worldwide."

"Hell. What does Harry make of it?"

"He seemed pretty shocked at first and it's thanks to

him we made it back to Centrum. Then he and Sarah Loveridge got really close and he's changed. He seems all for the Supreme Council and the Quota System now."

So I don't trust Boscombe. It's too much in his own interests. He can make as many passes as he likes but he's wasting his time. On the other hand, Harry did pair himself off with Sarah when we split two and two. Maybe it's wishful thinking on my part but I can't believe Harry believes in Quotas. He must be staying in Centrum to oppose them but Boscombe says otherwise.

Anton had no doubt about his duty to stay and help the dissidents. I will stay for now but need a sound plan to get to Centrum, survive and find out more. For the time being, I've resigned myself to a life of discomfort, worry and no congenial company.

We're called terrorists and rebels now as well as dissidents. More people have joined us and we've saved many genuine victims from hanging.

Max has his good points, I suppose. Today, we enjoyed running the gauntlet down in Felston wearing outlandish costumes for Summer Carnival.

We went into the Ploughshare to tip Kathy the wink and, before leaving town, saw a man named Simeon hanged in the public square.

FRANKENSTEIN ON THE MOON

Of course, Darren never expected to work for Frankenstein on the moon.

"The Lifetrap's developed a great deal since Nantoer, Doctor Redding," he said, crossing the laboratory to touch the gleaming contraption.

Darren always thought of the doctor as Frankenstein, Frank for short, but never called him either to his face.

"Call me Peter. We're very informal here. Of course it's developed and with your engineering skills it'll get even better but I hope Briony told you that we don't mention Nantoer here or the... er, old days."

Darren smiled. It made him sound like one of Frank's long time colleagues but, in fact, back then he'd been only a boy. At one time he'd felt extremely jealous of the older man's seemingly close association with Briony but not anymore. "Yes. Briony said. Sorry. As we're alone I thought it wouldn't matter."

As if to underline his indiscretion, a dark-haired, curvaceous woman entered the lab and paused theatrically on the threshold.

"Ah! Lady Balthazar," said Frank with a sardonic look on his face. "Our department is not often honoured with your presence."

"I heard you had a new member of staff, Peter. Norman asked me to make sure all the arrivals off the shuttle knew about his welcoming reception. And everyone else on the base, of course."

"How very thoughtful of the Director."

"And this is?" she asked, casting Darren a come-hither look.

"Darren Webster. Darren, meet Lady Balthazar."

"So formal. Call me Anna. And you, Peter. Just as you did at Nantoer."

Close up, her face belied the first impression of youthfulness. This was the woman Darren had been warned against. Briony called her Cruella de Vil, so when she smiled he saw the fixed grin of a shark.

Though Peter Redding didn't like others referring to Nantoer, when alone in his quarters, he often thought of his younger self and that difficult time.

His friend Jonathan Knight's last session on the prototype Lifetrap often filled his mind, Jon clambering groggily out of the hammock at the centre of a complex web of tubes and flexes of what they then jokingly called the deathtrap.

"How long?" Jonathan had asked.

"Twenty-four hours. Congratulations."

Jon smiled and looked round for Anna's approval.

"Where's Anna?"

"She shot off. Took your car. I don't know what got into her."

But he did. Anna was Jonathan's girl but acted in a very provocative manner towards Peter whenever Jon lay inert in suspension.

The previous night had been the worst. She was supposed to be monitoring Jon while Peter had his head down in the office. As he drifted off on the none-too-comfortable camp bed, Anna had slid in behind him, kissed his neck, caressed him. At first it seemed a pleasant dream but suddenly he was wide awake. He rolled off the bed, landing up on the floor.

"Don't, Anna! We can't leave Jon on the trap unsupervised."

"He's perfectly all right for half an hour."

Peter was aroused and desired her but wouldn't rock the boat. Not yet. Their team of three had to work together, had to succeed before time and luck ran out.

"No he's not, Anna. It's not on."

"It is, it is," she said and threw herself into his arms.

He kissed her passionately then pulled away and dragged himself to the monitor screens, trembling slightly.

"Time's short, Anna. Perhaps when the project's properly off the ground, I'll talk to Jonathan, sort something out. He's my friend as well as yours."

"I'll have probably grown very bored with this project by then," she said and flounced out.

Now, Jon hobbled through to the office, leaning on the walls for support.

Peter pulled aside one of the blinds and gazed through the grimy window at grass and weeds pushing through the tarmac of the parking area.

"We'll go back in my car. Feel able to walk that far?"

They always parked at the far end under the trees, close to the rutted lane which led down to a gate twined with barbed-wire.

"Just about," said Jon, holding onto the window ledge. "We ought to be testing round the clock. Anna should be going straight onto the trap."

"I think she's getting weary of it. You'll have to keep her sweet."

Jonathan smiled. "Of course! Hey, twenty-four hours!

Bet Anna will do thirty-six. Where some things are concerned, women are tougher than men."

Peter had already done forty-eight hours but didn't bother to remind him.

"Damn! Those bloody kids again!" He'd glimpsed a small figure disappearing behind straggly bushes. "It's going to be a big problem if they keep bunking over the perimeter fences."

"How many were there?" asked Jon.

"I only saw one but there may have been more. Hope they don't make the guys who walk the perimeter start poking about. We knew our own security would be a problem without staff. Strictly speaking we need domestic help, too, and lab assistants to monitor and record accurately. Getting Anna was a great bonus but I don't think she's been that fussy about entering all the readings."

"I expect she's had assistants to do all that for her in the big research organizations she's worked for."

Nantoer itself had been a huge establishment once, funded by the Defence Department with a top secret, high security rating. Defence cuts had meant a gradual run-down. Those terrestrial projects which survived had been transferred to other parts of the country and the aerospace schemes had been cancelled.

His own project continued unknown to the authorities, a desperate measure to try and complete the work. Peter had bribed the electrician to leave their supply on, persuaded the removal people that their department's equipment was being removed elsewhere at a later date and had duplicate keys cut before handing in his own. He knew it could only be short-term and would get him into terrible trouble if his stratagems were uncovered.

A security firm now monitored the site and a couple of men patrolled the perimeter but rarely made a close inspection of their end of the extensive grounds.

The laboratory, on the extreme edge of the furthest airfield and not visible from the main buildings, had once been a sports pavilion. In some golden age of plentiful funding, so much research was undertaken that it had been appropriated as extra work space though still referred to as The Pavilion. A veranda facing onto a bald, flat playing field ran the length of the building on the side opposite the car park. Woodland surrounded the rest of the building and its parking area.

They never showed a light. The glow of the monitor screen and torchlight were enough to work by in the largest room of the pavilion housing the lab. Its boarded-up windows suited the project. The window of the adjacent office had old vertical blinds which let in a little daylight.

Continuing was only possible because Peter's friend and colleague Doctor Jonathan Knight, their medical specialist, felt equally determined that they should succeed, equally convinced that they were close to the breakthrough.

"We said at the beginning it would be hard with only two of us. Having Anna has reduced some of the pressure," said Jonathan.

"True. But though she's a close friend of yours, Jon, I'm still not too sure of her loyalty. I think she really believes in the cryogenic solution to the problem."

"Well, that's her specialty but she's impressed with our higher temperature work."

"And I think she may just be collecting data that's useful to her own work and to Professor Balthazar in Cambridge."

"No, Pete, no. Anna's not like that."

"Certainly hope not. We have enough to contend with. Once the Defence Department's electricity bills get checked out, the whole thing could be blown. Either that or the locals will start talking."

"I told Tom at the Red Lion that we're part of security but more hush-hush than the official firm."

"That should soon get round the village, then."

"Tom also asked when we would pay last week's bed and breakfasts."

"I'll go into town soon and draw some more cash on my credit card." He sighed. His charge card would probably run out soon. "Feel ready to go back yet?"

Jon nodded. "And ready to eat so I must be better."

Outside, Peter checked around the building. He picked up some sweet wrappers from the veranda and found a small muddy footprint on the step of the locked side door which they never used.

The car ground down the steep track between high banks to the old sports club gates. Trees grew at dizzying angles, forming a dark tunnel. Beyond the sunken road, between the outcrops of rock and tangled thorn, the ground was spongy and treacherous. That and the frequent gales off Cardigan Bay howling up the drive probably discouraged the security firm's employees from patrolling too often at this end of the site. In theory, nothing of value remained, anyway.

"Damn. Anna left the gates open."

It was a nuisance undoing the padlock, driving through and getting out again to relock but they needed to for the sake of appearances.

When they got back Anna sat eating a meal in the empty lounge bar of the Red Lion.

Jonathan sat down and took her free hand. "You must've felt very hungry."

She glared balefully at Peter. "Food helps me when I've important decisions to make. With the impossible situation that's developed I was going to leave but I've decided to compromise. Providing there are no more deathtrap spells for me I'm prepared to stay. That's just what it is. A deathtrap."

"If you've so little faith in the project, why stay?" asked Peter. "Afraid you might miss useful stuff you can filch for your own work on cryonics?"

"Cryonics deals in dead tissue. My work is cryobiology, concerned with living tissue," she said haughtily. "There's nothing I can learn here which could be useful in my own field. I'm staying simply out of loyalty to Jonathan."

"Yes, I've noticed," said Peter. "You're very, very loyal."

Anna's glittering eyes gave him a look of pure hatred. He wondered how somebody could be so changeable, panting for love one minute and radiating waves of loathing the next.

"You really want to spend time working in the Balthazar Lab?" frowned Frankenstein. "Anna hasn't put pressure on you?"

"Well, she has," said Darren, "but it should be to our advantage. I shan't be disloyal to you. I'm on your side, Peter. It's only for a few hours a week but we'll have a foot in both camps."

"Okay. But watch out for Anna. She can be quite… persuasive."

When Peter regained consciousness he immediately registered the three-dimensional labyrinth of wires which both monitored and supplied his every need. Directly above his head a screen showed Jonathan at the control panel.

"I'm just going to key in your levels, Pete."

Jon's head disappeared and a chart took its place. On the end of a hospital bed it would be alarming, showing many vital activities as non-functional.

"Pretty impressive, huh? Now, here's your brain activity. Signs of frustration, I suspect, because you're at the stage where you can't communicate. We'll go into the YES/NO routine until speech function comes back."

The screen cleared.

"Okay, so there's not much to discuss. Anna's been sweet as pie. Think she'll probably go back on the trap if you apologise nicely for suggesting she's trying to steal our data. Okay? Will you do it?"

Peter tried to wriggle his right thumb to say YES but nothing appeared on screen. With feeling oozing back, he began to experience pins and needles and weird itching sensations. The ability to move and communicate would come back gradually but with it pain. Peter shut his eyes and longed for the day when these problems were ironed out.

"Oh-oh, here comes Anna. Try and manage a little groan to prove we men suffer for our science."

Peter's left thumb inadvertently twitched NO and the screen surprised him with its negative, which always spread across the whole of the monitor.

"Ah, feeling a bit bolshie, eh? Well, the trap's enough to make anyone tetchy at times. Never mind, my turn next."

"Oh no it's not."

The screen cleared and Anna's face appeared wearing a slightly malignant smile. "I've a good mind to make him stay in limbo forever."

Anna's words seared a pang of fear through Peter's chest and abdomen.

"Anna, what've you got against the poor guy?" asked Jon. "Give him a break. It's my turn tomorrow and, believe it or not, I'm looking forward to it."

"Ah!" she said. "And what do you think Peter and I will be doing?"

"Monitoring me pretty damn carefully, I hope."

"Oh no. We'll be in bed. If he had his way."

"Come on. You're hallucinating. Peter wouldn't look at you twice."

Both men saw the dangerous glint in her eye, Peter through the monitor, Jonathan face to face.

Jon hastily amended his statement, "Sure enough, Pete probably finds you very attractive but he's too loyal to do anything."

"Yes? Is that why he's always pestering me?"

"Peter, are you always pestering Anna?"

Feeling was back. He managed an immediate NO.

"Of course, he's bound to tell you."

"Look, Anna, I believe him. He's my oldest friend."

"You'd rather believe him and make me a liar?"

"Well, no, but…"

"He kissed me."

"Peter, did you kiss Anna?"

The machine didn't allow "Yes, but…", only YES or NO. Peter hesitated.

"Kind of a long delay, don't you think?" said Anna.

"It's difficult at this stage when the feeling's only just returning."

"Well, the answer's 'yes' and I'm sick of it," she shouted. "Just leave him on the deathtrap for all time."

"Anna, that would scuttle our whole scheme. Without systematic testing we'll never be able to prove the trap is practical and efficient, safer and more viable than cryogenics."

"I don't think that'll ever happen. There are better systems and they need to be set up somewhere where we'll be appreciated, at a site with proper facilities not a ramshackle outfit like this. Read this, Jon. I've negotiated a really good deal for us and the fact that I've believed in the cryobiological solution all along has to help."

She flashed the letter, headed Cambridge Research/

Government Funding, in front of the screen for Peter to glimpse.

"This is a fantastic offer," said Jon, studying it more closely. "Is Balthazar really on the level?"

"Of course. He's got official backing and needs capable people to prove cryogenics can work. Let's capitalise on it. My work on suspended animation has been frittered away here. With this scheme it could make real progress."

She threw a switch on the equipment.

"Anna! Don't do that! Whatever we decide, Pete's part of the team."

"Maybe." She directed a venomous glance at Peter. "But he can stay there while we discuss it in private."

"I'll be back, Pete," muttered Jon, hurrying after Anna who had stalked huffily through the door.

All kinds of clichés ran through Peter's head. The fury of a woman scorned came to mind and the one about the guy who lusted after his best friend's girl. He'd done the decent thing, resisted, and for what?

He heard their raised voices outside. A car door slammed followed by an engine firing, a shout of 'Anna!' as it accelerated away.

Now Jon would come and take him off the damn loop she'd set. But, no. Another car door, a further engine burst, more violent acceleration.

Time stretched endlessly for Peter, alternating between oblivion and spells of consciousness and pain. For brief moments he had the power of speech but nobody to converse with. Then the serum automatically kicked in, spreading through his bloodstream and the cycle began again. For one individual, the reservoir in use at present could last four years he calculated in one of his waking periods.

After what seemed a week, Jonathan returned.

"How long?" Peter asked.

"Three days. I'm sorry."

"It can work. That's the record. It will improve. Make Anna see sense."

"There's no moving her. You've really upset her."

"That's crazy!" Speaking was getting difficult. The ability would soon be gone again. "She was throwing herself at me, not the other way around."

"Sorry, I can't believe that."

"And she's put the machine on a loop. For God's sake take me out of it."

"We're moving to Cambridge to work on cryogenics. Anna will want to see you're still here before we go which creates a problem. If the deathtrap's still working, Anna will consider it dangerous opposition to her work. She'll be tempted to leave you to enjoy your own system for as long as it lasts. I'm planning to come back later to release you but you've been such a scab I might just be tempted to ignore my feelings of humanity."

Peter tried to speak but managed only a croak.

"Anna says even if the deathtrap worked, it would put the subjects at grave risk, leaving them vulnerable to outside influence. Trapped, in fact. Makes you think, huh?"

"That applies to cryogenics, too," Peter managed to mumble.

But the door had slammed, the key turned.

"I hope you freeze in hell!" he shouted but it came out as a slurred burble.

Peter existed. Days stretched. The deathtrap sustained his life. Once he'd suggested that they adapt their tongue-in-cheek name and call the equipment the Lifetrap. That's what it was proving to be.

Both Anna and Jon appeared to him next but Peter wasn't sure if they were dream, hallucination or reality.

"It's working surprisingly well so far," said Anna. "We'll

leave him to his success. Or otherwise."

"How long?" groaned Peter, deciding they were real.

"Six more days," said Jon. "We're leaving today."

They left. Peter lay stretched in a loop of alternating states of oblivion and awareness, proving his system's viability but knowing it ensured he would never be released.

"Climate change is still causing concern," said Frank, scanning the newspapers which had arrived on the shuttle that morning. He passed them across the desk to Darren.

"The tabloids seem to be making much of it. Scaremongering and pointing the finger. 'Global warming could be the end of us all while scientists fiddle in safety on the moon'."

"Scumbags. Which reminds me. Did you hear Sir George didn't arrive as expected?"

"Yes. Wonder why."

"He's got a heart condition, they say, but I suspect Cruella told him not to come so she can continue to twist Norman Metcalfe round her little finger and get away with murder for Balthazar Labs."

Peter surfaced to sounds of scuffling.

"Look at this geezer, Briony."

Two grimy children stared at him in the half-light from the door.

"Spooky. What's he doing?"

"Not a lot," giggled the boy.

Peter tried to say, "Help to get me off the machine. I'll tell you how." Only a strange gargle emerged from his mouth.

The boy made a small, involuntary sound of fear and leapt away. "He's a Frankenstein monster or an alien. Come on, let's get out."

From the corner of his eye Peter saw him grasp the girl's arm and tug. She glanced back before being hauled from view. They probably left by way of the office window.

The complications would be horrendous once these kids told their parents and the parents informed the police but he'd be saved. Maybe even adverse publicity could be turned to the advantage of the Lifetrap. That was its name now. He'd survived with minimal sustenance. For how long? Peter began the impossible task of trying to work it out but blackness overtook him.

"Did George turn up on yesterday's shuttle?" asked Frank.

"No. What did arrive were loads of crates of deep frozen heads and bodies from Balthazar Laboratories."

"How can they get away with that? That's commercial work. It costs a small fortune anyway so I bet they're charging tenfold for clients to be stored in the comparative safety of Luna."

"Everyone's ganging up on Norman but he's got an answer for everything where Anna Balthazar's concerned. The power of lust, eh? Our dear Director says it's one of many essential aspects of the research."

Frank laughed. "What? Lust?"

"No," grinned Darren, "disgusting, useless, frozen stiffs."

"The Americans and the biosphere team won't let them get away with it, surely? Have you met their boss, Ed Young?"

"Yes. Had a drink with him the other day. When I told him my girlfriend's name for Lady Balthazar was Cruella, he laughed and said, 'I call her the Vamp but not to her face'."

"I hope you didn't go into Briony's original connection with Anna."

"No, of course not. Anyway, they're up in arms about it, say they don't see why they should be crapping themselves to provide resources just so the Balthazars can line their pockets. Apparently, Young's talking about withdrawing funding and all cooperation. Don't think my firm'll be too pleased, either, when they hear. They'll probably recall me."

"Damn."

Consciousness again. He opened his eyes.

"Hello," said a voice.

Had it been possible, Peter would have jumped.

The girl came within his view.

Hello. His mouth opened but nothing emerged.

"Can't you talk?"

"Soon!" It came out in a rush but Peter thought he'd said it.

"Darren's gone to the pictures. He said we'd better not come here again or tell anyone about it. He's scared. I was too but…" Her voice trailed off. "If his dad knew he'd been up here, he'd give him a hiding. My dad wouldn't." The child paused. "My mum would though. But she says you ought to help people."

Twitching his thumb, a big YES spread onto the screen above him. Peter tried to nod towards it but his head wouldn't move.

The girl stepped a little nearer, taking in the maze of wires and connections, touching one tentatively before quickly withdrawing her hand.

"Wish I was a scientist."

"You can…" She turned her head sharply, so he'd managed some kind of sound. "You – can…"

"Can what?"

To say, "Be a scientist" was beyond him. Peter shut his eyes then tried again.

"I - can - speak - soon. Look at - screen." She glanced around. "Above - me."

As the girl edged closer, moving warily among loops of flex, Peter twitched his thumb. 'Yes' spread across the screen. She flinched slightly then said, "Oh". Movement coming back fast, he quickly flicked 'No'.

"What's it for?"

"Comm - un - ee…"

"Communication."

YES.

"Great. I'll ask you some questions. Does one and one make two?"

YES.

"What's my…? No, that's no good. It's only 'yes' or 'no'. Is my name Briony?"

He remembered the boy calling to her. YES.

"Good! Can I speak Welsh?"

She didn't sound like a native of these parts. NO.

"Wrong!"

Of course, they all learnt it at school. Kids soon picked it up.

"*Bore da.*" He could speak!

"*P'nawn da*, silly."

Afternoon, not morning. "Good afternoon, Briony." She sidled away. "Will you get me - off this machine? I'll be able - to talk - soon. It's - my machine but some bad people - put me on it. Can't escape without help." He gulped for air. "You have to be quick - before I fall asleep again."

"Okay."

"Walk up the ramp. Look at the monitor screens. You've used computers?"

"Yes, course I have."

"Here's me twitching YES with my thumb. Is it showing on a screen?"

"Yes."

"Good. Everything should work then. To the right of the keyboard is a metal switch like a big handle. It's quite stiff. Can you turn it for me?"

"Which way?"

"Towards you."

He heard her grunting and the scuffing of her feet. "It won't move."

Damn. She was just a child. Her wrist wasn't strong enough.

"I can hear a car," said Briony. "Is it the bad people coming back?"

"It might be. Try both hands." Peter could hear her panting. "Any luck?"

Now he could hear the car himself, grinding up to the top of the track. "You'd better go. Don't let anyone catch you here."

There was a sudden click. "Done it!"

It might be too late.

"Help me with the buckle on this headband then go." Peter whipped off wires and sensor pads, aware of the car's tyres crunching to a halt at the far end of the car park.

"Quick. Through here."

He practically tripped over the camp bed in the office, ignored the small gap in the window and propelled Briony through the far door into a tiled passage. There were only two further doors, one to the toilets and showers, the other the side exit with its key on the inside. They stumbled through.

"Shut it," gasped Peter.

A car door slammed.

"Over here," whispered Briony and they crawled behind tangled bushes which bordered the path surrounding the pavilion.

The child moved away, silent on old smooth-soled canvas shoes.

Peter lay down and shut his eyes. Leaving the Lifetrap at such speed before any proper recovery time had completely exhausted him.

Another door slammed and he heard Anna's voice.

"Hurry up, Jon. We don't want to be here all day."

"I've no stomach for it, Anna."

"He'll be dead. You don't have to do anything. We just have to be sure. Somebody else will find him. Just a mad scientist with a crazy scheme who, fortunately, killed himself rather than others."

"If he's alive, I'm taking him off."

"Not if I can help it. Doctor Jonathan Knight, a man of such talent and promise. Think how being struck off might ruin your career."

"Fuck my career."

"Fraudulent use of government property, certainly. Attempted murder by default. That's not allowed under the Hippocratic oath, surely?"

"Shut up!"

Peter could hear shoes crunching on the gravel and then the main door being unlocked. Soon after, their raised voices could be heard inside, altercations and questions, but no distinct words.

They were outside again.

"Anna! What are you doing?"

"You'll see."

Her rapid footsteps receded and returned, followed by smashing and crashing sounds from within, then Anna's voice outside again. "We should set it on fire."

"Don't be ridiculous," said Jon wearily. "We don't want smoke drawing attention to the place. Let's get back to Cambridge and let vandals get the blame. Some other vandals."

After the car left, Briony crawled back and sat beside Peter.

"Do you really want to be a scientist?"

The girl grinned, as if used to people making ironic jokes but he'd been serious. "Who was that lady?" she asked.

"That was no lady…" said Peter with a bitter smile. "Anna's a scientist but you wouldn't turn out like her."

Briony disappeared into the building but returned very rapidly and slumped down beside him again. "She got a spanner from the car and smashed everything up. The man used a bad word but seemed nicer than her. He didn't really want to do anything wicked."

"No. That's true. But he did."

"Norman's talking about cutting funds to this department. Are the Balthazar's threatened too?"

"No," said Darren. "Cruella's trying to talk him into giving them more. I don't know why she confides in me. She's always trying to get me to leave you and work for them full-time and must have convinced herself that eventually I will."

"And will you?"

"Certainly not. This is the work I'm committed to and Cruella's an absolute bitch. She's bad-mouthing our department left, right and centre so that our loss can be their gain. Besides which, you're not all that bad to work for."

Frank sighed. "Wish I'd been totally dishonest when Norman originally asked me to contact Balthazar Labs. I might have said they had too much other work, that they weren't interested, anything. Unfortunately, I'm not built that way."

"Sorry, Doctor Redding, Sir George won't be in until tomorrow morning. Can anyone else help? Lady Balthazar's here."

"I had no idea Sir George had remarried. Is Lady Balthazar *au fait* with the work of the Laboratories then?"

"Oh yes. She's the former deputy, Doctor Anna Torrington."

"Ah! Yes. I'd better speak to Sir George in the morning. Tell me, is Doctor Jonathan Knight still on your staff?"

There was a long pause. "No, I'm afraid not."

"You mean you didn't know?" asked Briony in amazement.

"Not about the marriage," said Peter. "I knew he'd been knighted."

When on leave, Peter always tried to visit his protégée, Briony Clarke, on campus and take her out to lunch.

"So did you speak to Lady Balthazar?"

"No. I'll phone George tomorrow. He's not so bad."

"Deluded by Cruella, no doubt, but not so bad."

"Norman Metcalfe's trying to rope in everyone who might contribute. There's a tremendous sense of urgency with the climate change problems. The first small satellite community has been launched from the moon but, of course, it's very experimental. I'm not that keen on involving Balthazar but feel obliged to make contact."

"I wouldn't!"

"And there'll always be a place for you, Briony, when you graduate."

She smiled. "Thanks. I'll probably get some experience down here first."

"How's the study going?"

"Finals are a bit of a strain on the nerves but fingers crossed."

"You'll be fine. How are your parents?"

"Okay. They're beginning to appreciate what you've done for me, I think."

Peter's help and encouragement with her education

had caused friction between Briony and her parents at times. They felt he encouraged her to grow away from them and couldn't believe that his input came with no strings attached. In fact, he was a little in love with her but felt unable to act. The age gap wouldn't have bothered him but confirming her parents' nasty accusations would.

"Can I come and use your reference library after lunch?" Peter asked.

"Of course. They'll be quite chuffed that the great Doctor Peter Redding wants to use their facilities."

He laughed. "That sounds like somebody famous, not me! Anyway, I'm only wanting to use the current BMA listing. I want to trace Jonathan Knight."

"Oh. Cruella's sidekick. Why's that?"

"I'm going to offer him a job."

"Magnanimous."

"Not necessarily. Not everyone thinks working on the moon a great option but he had so much background and experience of the biological problems, I could do with his help and so could some of the other projects."

"You probably didn't see it, but a couple of years ago there was a lot in the papers about him going missing. I kept some cuttings. If you like we can pick them up from my room before you go back."

After lunch they strolled through the campus to the university library. Jon wasn't listed in the current British Medical Association Yearbook. The librarian insisted on checking the online listing, too, but there was nothing.

They continued to the untidy terraced house, which Briony shared with four others. On the way up to her room he was introduced to two of them.

"Not engineering undergrads by any chance, are they? I'm also looking for a good practical engineer but they're like gold dust."

"No but I know a good engineer."

"Do you?"

"Darren."

"Not the one who…?"

She nodded. "Darren Webster."

"Thought he worked in a garage."

"He did. We always meet in the Red Lion when I'm back in Nantoer and I think me being at uni encouraged Darren to get some qualifications of his own. Anyway, he works for Fugu Electronics now."

"Fugu are already doing work for us. Maybe I'll follow that up."

Briony rooted around in drawers and folders until she found the cuttings about the disappearance of Jonathan Knight.

"Of course, Anna threw him over for Balthazar," said Peter. "Perhaps Jon decided to make a completely fresh start somewhere else."

"Maybe. But my theory is he knew too much about Cruella's murky past and he's in one of those great big milk crates."

"Milk crates?"

"One of their containers for so-called cryonic preservation. You watch your back, Peter, if she joins you on the moon."

"The gutter press are enjoying themselves, as usual. 'Global instability is affecting whole populations and threatening more with drought and earthquake, flood and volcanic eruption while scientists and technicians scuttle off to the moon like rats leaving the sinking ship'."

"Bloody stupid tabloids."

"Never mind, Darren. We'll ban all their scummy journalists from the satellite cities when the time comes."

"They can't imagine what it's like cut off from someone

you love and not being able to drink with your mates in a friendly pub."

"True, the Luna Bar does lack a certain atmosphere."

Frank continued to sort through the rest of the mail.

"Anyone interesting arrive on this shuttle?" he asked.

"No. Only more frozen stiffs. And still no Briony. I enjoy my work but... Well, tell you the truth, I'd started to make it with her and, in some respects, the last thing I'd wanted was to piss off to the moon. If Fugu insist on me returning it could be for the best. I might get to see her again."

"Look, be patient, Darren. I'm sure she won't be able to resist the offer. After all, like you, she was in near the very start of this project, in fact, saved it from being snuffed out altogether. Anyway, if you go, how the hell am I going to cope with Anna?"

"Huh! Ignore the bitch."

"Hey! Hold on! Here it is. Briony's accepted the post."

Darren's face broke into a broad smile. "Really?"

"She's working notice on her current project and will be arriving on the next shuttle."

"Wonderful!"

"Only another three months," Frank added.

"More streamlined than the first time we saw it," laughed Briony. "Lots of Lifetraps, too, in parallel. How many?"

Darren grinned and strode down the line proprietorially. "Ten. And it'll be extended to ten rows in depth soon."

"A hundred! I see there are several guinea pigs. Who are they?"

"They're volunteers who answered our adverts. Some can't wait to get off the planet, others are sad cases, derelicts, bankrupts. They get a salary but oblivion is all they want. This woman lost all her family in a car smash. Now she's in a coma of our making but we can revive her whenever we wish."

"Impressive. And what's the situation with Cruella? I saw her from afar at the reception."

"Yes, she usually only chats up the men. Still manipulating. Cruella's a pain in the arse so far as this department's concerned. Our work's going really well but, unfortunately, she's got Norman Metcalfe eating out of her hand and she's still trying to do down Frank at every turn and keep herself and Balthazar on top."

"Remember Jonathan Knight?"

"No but you've told me plenty about him. Is he still missing?"

"Yes. I think he's up here. Cruella put Peter on the Lifetrap to sink or swim all those years ago. It seems natural that if she wanted Jonathan out of the way she'd use her system."

"You mean among all the bodies in the freezing-bins waiting for their resurrection into a better world? Why here among hundreds when down at Balthazar Labs it could be lost among thousands?"

"It's less accessible to the police or anyone else who might be interested."

"Who else would be?"

"The police came up with nothing so the family hired a private investigator, I discovered, but there's a big gap when he was working at Nantoer."

Darren gave a sardonic smile. "We're not supposed to use that name here."

"Yes, I know. Knight worked at Balthazar's until he disappeared so the detective would have been making enquiries there about that blank period. I think that's when Cruella decided he must come up here."

"It's just a theory."

"Yes but worth looking into."

"Oh, no, Briony. Don't. Cruella's much too dangerous a woman to mess with."

Briony shrugged. "We'll see."

Briony slipped into Balthazar Labs' storage area to continue her search. It was her third visit. Darren had reluctantly told her how to unscrew and check out the vats. So far she'd ignored the small bins containing heads. If her theory was correct then it seemed likely that Anna had wanted to dispose of a whole body.

Since her one brief childhood glimpse of Jonathan Knight she'd seen only press photos. Protective gloves on, Briony paused over many male faces wondering whether he might have metamorphosed thus.

Then she found herself staring into his face; a pallid, ghastly visage with a fixed stare but definitely him. Drawing in her breath sharply, Briony pulled a marker pen from her overalls and made a cross out of view at the back of the container then, dry ice swirling around her, began to refasten the lid.

"Make sure you close it properly, Miss Clarke," said a sharp voice.

She whirled round to find Anna Balthazar staring stonily, hands on hips.

"I believe that's a particular friend of mine who asked for complete secrecy regarding his whereabouts and about the untreatable cancer he was suffering."

"Poor man. He must have been lucky to have you for a friend, Lady Balthazar."

"Don't play the sarcastic bitch with me, girl, or you might find you have medical complications that need the same solution."

She stepped forward and gave Briony a sudden vicious

punch on the nose. Briony fell backwards straight-legged, like an off-balance toddler in a play-pen. Anna leapt forward, pulling a hypodermic from her lab coat and plunged it into the younger woman's neck. Briony screamed and started to struggle to her feet then fell back, the world spiralling above her, strange voices echoing around the dark vortex until everything merged into blackness.

"She was hoist by her own petard."

"Will anybody ever find her?"

Darren laughed. "There's been quite a hue and cry but nobody has so far."

"How did you reach me so quickly?" asked Briony.

"Every time you went to Balthazar's storage I'd follow and make sure everything went to plan."

"I don't know how to thank you," sighed Briony.

"Yes you do."

She smiled and kissed him.

"I wanted to return to Earth," said Darren, "but it might look suspicious if she's found."

"Return to Earth? Everyone else is clamouring to come to the moon."

"Yes. But I miss real life and pubs."

"I know the Earth looks wonderful from up here but down there everything's changed. There's no community life left. You'd do better to start your own bar here. As the interchange for the satellites, it should get busier and busier. You'll make a fortune."

He laughed. "If you stay, I'll stay, working as Frank's engineer. Incidentally, I'm sure Knight's dead although Cruella put him with the cryogenics."

"They're still alive?"

"According to her classification, yes. The others, the cryonics, are goners, waiting for a miracle and huge advancements in medicine."

"So the cryogenics are like Frank's subjects and could be reanimated?"

"That's the theory but I've seen no proof. It'll probably be the Lifetrap which saves the human race. The satellites can only take so many. Eventually, people will reach new planets thanks to Frankenstein."

"And us," smiled Briony. "We've both made our contribution since way, way back."

Darren chuckled, hugging her to him.

"Where is Cruella exactly?"

"I'm not a murderer, you'll be glad to know. She's in the cryogenics, too. Just behind Knight."

"So, if they find her, she could be revived and might testify against us."

"Only if the system's as good as she claims. But I'm not too worried. How about you?"

"About her or your morals?"

"Both."

"I'm not in the least bit worried," said Briony, kissing him tenderly. "She's hoist."

FEAR OF THE ALIEN

Monitors picked up the craft which hurtled into the planet's atmosphere. After a couple of turns around the surface at high speed it was seen to make physical contact above a dense and widespread forest. Racing at a manic rate over the dark expanse, the ship skimmed the roof of the jungle with an intermittent clattering, then bounced rhythmically on an ocean of foliage like a stone skipping across water. Twigs and branches snapped with rapid pistol shots as metal scraped and screeched, tearing a path through the treetops.

A gap in the jungle appeared and the vessel's forward motion ceased.

The watchers lost visual contact as it turned a double somersault to plummet into a sloping rocky clearing below. The final smash and uncontrollable sideways slide, accompanied by horrific rending noises eventually dying to silence, went undetected.

Major Karlon became conscious first of pain then lack of sound: no engine hum, no motion. They must have landed. But where? Memory of the crippled battlecruiser came flooding back.

After decades of drills it seemed unbelievable that the hoarse blare of klaxons meant a real Abandon Ship.

Boots had thudded to the lifecraft in haste but without panic. Karlon's vessel with no missing, no casualties, quickly closed hatches and span through the pitch-black

Escape Screw to be expelled from the body of the spaceship.

Looking back, instead of the gleaming yellow-striped fighting ship of Emergency Drills, they saw a blackened, blistered hull ripped open in a dozen places to reveal whole decks twisted, shattered or obliterated.

At the controls, Lieutenant Dorlim zig-zagged them away from the stricken vessel. Karlon used the forward cannon to deflect all kinds of detritus threatening progress while crew fired on their enemies from the side ports. Cheers could be heard to stern where Trant, the rear gunner, mopped up some more dangerous stuff on their tail.

Ahead Karlon saw the remains of a deck spread out like a miniature asteroid belt. From a distance the debris formed a bright, nursery-wall pattern against the dark backdrop of space but he knew that closer inspection would make unpleasant viewing.

"Let's avoid this, Lieutenant."

"It'd be camouflage, Major."

Karlon hesitated. "Okay."

Unoccupied spacesuits floated forlornly. The craft negotiated snaking cables and pipe, display panels, video tape, a twisted locker streaming underwear. They slid past all manner of messes, mostly organic, causing much vomiting in the main cabin.

Karlon realised they were no longer under power.

"I didn't ask you to cut engine, Lieutenant."

"No, Major, but it'll be safer to drift for a while."

"In fact, this is the last place we want to linger." He could still hear retching from the cabin and his own system felt like resonating in sympathy.

"Hey, Major. There's someone alive in that suit," roared the rear gunner.

There was silence.

"Quick, we could fire a lifecord or I'll go out on a line myself," shouted Trant.

The two officers exchanged looks and shook their heads.

"Major! Lieutenant! We gotta do something!"

Karlon could almost feel the wave of disapproval from behind the cockpit division.

"Stay alert at your posts, men," he murmured. "We're going to move slow ahead."

Their craft emerged on the other side of the smashed deck, well-screened from the battle. Under Dorlim's sure touch they gradually drifted to a kind of safety. Death under fire receded but, before long, everyone realised that they were adrift in the vastness of space with limited life-support.

Within hours Karlon had to come to terms with the navigational computer being first unreliable, then non-functional.

Dorlim saw the planet first and ever after claimed it as his own.

"Love at first sight," muttered Trant.

"Look," whispered Dorlim, as they drew nearer. "It shimmers like a jewel."

Trant's laugh crackled nervously on the intercom.

"All that glitters is not good."

Dorlim, however, would hear nothing against his new love.

"I'll get us to that planet," he muttered, gritting his teeth, "if it's the last thing I do."

"Fine," said Karlon. "It's our only chance of survival anyway."

"Let's hope there's decent food and drink down there. And a soft bed," said Buttlinger from the belly of the vessel.

"And soft women," another voice added.

"Remember what I said," warned Trant, "all that glitters…"

"And how about a spacecraft repair hangar with a spare anti-matter overdrive to get us back to Panavell," laughed a different voice, which Karlon recognised as Sheen's.

"Or better still with a newly constructed Super-Constell Cruiser on the rig," said Buttlinger.

"Ready to go," cackled Sheen.

"You won't want any of that," crooned Dorlim. "You'll want to stay when you get there, put down roots, forget war and S-C Cruisers, missiles and K Food."

Karlon thought that would be as well. The chances of rescue, once down, seemed remote but the crew were buoyant. Perhaps that was the reason for Dorlim's enthusiasm, a ploy to keep them in good heart.

The planet had gradually increased in size and become no less beautiful.

"I wouldn't be at all surprised if this were a friendly planet, a neutral," said Dorlim.

"Why a neutral? Why not an ally?" asked Sheen.

"Because they'd tip us into a spare cruiser and send us back to the battle," muttered Trant.

"This planet desires us. It's got a pull," said Dorlim.

"A pull?" said Karlon in alarm.

"Magnetic, I think. It's reeling us in. Our little beat-up pod couldn't do this speed on her own."

"Let's hope she can stand the strain. How are the heat shields on these craft?"

"Automatic," Dorlim replied, "and good, so I've heard."

"They'll need to be with this velocity."

Those were their last words. Karlon's eyes closed, remembering the demented looping of the planet, his fear that the lifecraft would break up, closely followed by the horror of knowing nothing could forestall their imminent crash-landing. Dorlim's loud, long-drawn-out howl as he wrenched at the controls filled his head then faded as conscious mind drifted into nothingness.

Karlon jerked into wakefulness again. As senior officer, he must monitor the situation, make decisions and translate them into action.

Despite the insufferable heat in the cabin, none of the instrument panels glowed. There was no power, no information, no oxygen.

No oxygen! He made to leap up. His upper body moved forward athletically but halted, statuesque, as pain seared through both legs. Breath held and every muscle tensed in order to bear the agony of the movement, Karlon fell back panting and sweating.

With face furrowed and lips pulled taut over teeth, one hand crept to push the emergency services button beside the seat. Nothing happened. No doubt everything smashed up on impact, even the emergency circuits.

All movement seemed to scourge his legs. Carefully he turned to observe the cockpit.

Dorlim lay dead, blood and gore spattering the control panel where his head had struck. The pilot should have been strapped tight for landing but had loosened the belts to cope more effectively with the vessel's crazy bucketing.

Releasing his own tags made no difference to Karlon. The front of the craft had stove in forward of the co-pilot's position, trapping his legs in a pincer of steelite.

He called out, "Trant! Sheen! Buttlinger!"

No reply. Nothing worked. Without intercom, no sound could penetrate the insulated door to the main cabin, firmly shut and out of reach.

"Trant! Sheen!"

Nothing.

"Buttlinger!"

Total silence.

"Anybody!"

With no other help available he determined to free himself. Karlon tugged at the compressed mass until sickening pain made him stop and close his eyes. Reopened, they focused on Dorlim's head, making him vomit at the sight of the repulsive mess.

Perspiration rolled from every sweat gland as he flopped back against his headrest. Feeling ill and exhausted, Karlon lapsed once more into sleep.

On regaining consciousness, a brighter light filtered through the cabin transparency above. Happiness engulfed him. His brain, though in no state to be analytical, soon deduced the reason for the sense of well-being. A comforting hum filled the cabin. Trant or somebody had become mobile enough to get some kind of life support working.

"Trant," he croaked. "Buttlinger. In the cockpit!"

No reply.

Sudden silence made him decide that the noise could not be the continuous, pervasive sound of an operational vessel.

Within seconds the noise began again, seeming to come from beyond Dorlim.

Something dark and hideous rose up behind the pilot's body. Karlon gazed in unbelieving horror.

The creature darted back behind Dorlim then immediately reappeared beside the lieutenant's head. Karlon drew out the handgun nestling in the seat pocket but felt unable to fire. If he hit the pilot's head, gunge and fragments of skull would fly all over him. Also, going against the rules irked him. Firearms should not be discharged within a vessel except in the direst emergency because of the risk to crew and equipment through ricochet. But this might be dire enough. The alien revolted him and the lifecraft was wrecked. Probably nobody but himself would be at risk. If the animal moved clear of Dorlim he would shoot.

A tic began to quiver his left eye-lid as sweat cascaded over his brows. The creature rose and Karlon tried to aim but the being's lightning speed and continual ducking and weaving thwarted him.

Vanished as suddenly as it reappeared, the silence was as frightening as the sound. Until it started up behind him.

Trapped by the legs, Karlon sat rigid with tension, unable to turn, knowing his adversary leapt and dived behind him rendering the handgun useless.

Suddenly, the alien hove into view and fell upon him. He shrieked and fired. The monstrosity pulled away only to bound back. Shot after frantic shot had no effect.

Powerless, eyes widening in fear, Karlon felt the alien's flesh upon his. As the creature began to insinuate itself against him, he tried to leap up, only to cause himself searing pain.

The thing sprang off but Karlon's heart lurched with dread as several others appeared and began to move about the cabin. They seemed to be attracted by Dorlim's body. As Karlon lay helpless, hopeless, the creatures congregated around the wound on the pilot's head, appearing to drink his blood.

A groan escaped him, reflecting both repugnance and pain. He sat upright and tried again to extricate himself from the mangled nose-cone. Teeth clamped together, tugging for as long as was bearable, the agony soon made the effort too terrible to sustain. The handgun proved useless as a lever, being too short, squat and smooth and, stretch as he might, nothing else could be reached. Even if free, his legs would probably be smashed and useless like the lifecraft.

Panting, sweating, feeling sick, Karlon sank back into the co-pilot's seat.

Sounds penetrated from outside, making him realise that the craft's external sensor's must be on. Clicks and tappings, snorts and snuffles, agonised wails and echoing howls filled the cabin. What was this place that Dorlim had been so eager to reach only to die in the effort?

He angled the co-pilot seat to avoid looking upon the plunder of Dorlim's body and found himself staring through the cockpit canopy. Lying inert, eyes open but unseeing, a sudden awareness zapped his mind. A great gash in the transparency yawned, allowing unknown and probably toxic atmosphere to penetrate the craft. Though still alive, the thought of obnoxious gases polluting the air in his lungs made him feel queasy.

Eyes still fixed on the fractured canopy, heartbeat beginning to steady, he groaned as aliens began to pour through the gap.

The vessel had been breached, something he should have realised long since. Heart beating faster than ever, Karlon drew the handgun and fired rapidly at the gap. The invasion ceased.

Crowds of the repulsive creatures already inside still jostled for position around Dorlim. Karlon let fly with the gun again just above the pilot's bloody pate until all the intruders had gone.

Turning back to the canopy, further bursts made no difference. Aliens began to swarm through the hole.

Badly in need of support, his voice grated feebly calling for Trant, increased in strength croaking for Sheen then managed a full-bodied scream.

"Buttlinger!"

The screeching crescendo sent the creatures racing round the cabin in a mad, dizzying frenzy. Aliens filled the cockpit, making contact as they passed, always unerringly going for his bare face and hands. Grappling for gloves and helmet, panic rose within him.

"Trant! Buttlinger!"

With trembling fingers, he drew on gauntlets from the seat-pouch then stretched in desperation for his helmet on the shelf above. The vice-like grip which held him meant Karlon could do no more than brush his fingertips against its reflective curve. He gripped the gun and sobbed. Aliens would penetrate and pollute him, fall upon his vulnerable face, suck moisture from his eyeballs and, working through the optic nerve, infiltrate his brain. Already they broached his sweating brow and cheeks, making them prickle.

He began shrieking. From the pit of his stomach, the sound invaded his whole being. Mouth wide, eyes squeezed into deep crow's feet, neck muscles taut, the scream that was Karlon filled the cockpit and spilled through the gash in the canopy out into the jungle beyond.

Gratings and sobs became incorporated in the main harmonic which became higher, louder, hoarser then suddenly, without warning, stopped.

As the scream died, a vehicle whispered down to land in the clearing.

Captain Otis, the pilot, together with her rescue party jumped to the ground and ran to the jagged hole which gaped in the crashed vessel's stern. The craft rocked as Otis led the way through the gap, handgun drawn.

Doctor Alban dragged his bulk along in the team's wake, mopping his glowing face with a huge handkerchief. Beside him, tall and pale, walked his new assistant.

"You see what I mean about lack of equipment, Richards. These craft always seem to crash in the most inaccessible places. Trying to find this one has been like looking for a louse in a labyrinth."

"The ambulance is old but it seems to incorporate a lot of modern technology."

"Well, we have cannibalised crashed vessels whenever possible. That helps."

"Ready for the day when…?"

"Quite so."

"And you have the technical know-how?"

"We have a lot of people with resourceful minds, let's say. We also have grateful technicians from off-planet whose lives we've saved."

Otis waited impatiently at the breach in the stern and helped pull Alban aboard.

"The guy on the rear armament was still alive. I've already sent him back to the bus."

"Good. You take the left side, Richards, I'll take the right."

They began to work forward along the central gangway, administering to the few survivors before sending them back to the ambulance.

The captain preceded them, gun at the ready.

"Does Otis have to wave that thing about?" Richards asked mildly.

"It's prudent. Crashed fighting men have been known to attack those intending to help them. Notice anything at all striking about this craft, Captain Otis?"

"It's damned hot. Even hotter than outside. And it stinks."

"That's true. What else?"

"It's small but I suppose it's a lifecraft rather than a main vessel."

"I'm sure you're right but what struck me was the all-male crew. Didn't see any markings but I'll bet this is a Panavellan ship."

"So?"

"When I do manage to get a few new patients, they

prove to be a bunch of war-mongering, treacherous fascisti who torture their enemies if there's information to be extorted and exterminate them if not."

"Huh. Sounds a bit like our Powers-That-Be. Makes me feel sorry for them. They're only the Poor Bloody Infantry, after all. But I'm sure you'll overcome your prejudices and treat them like any other patients."

"Not prejudice, fact. – Here's another one. Stretcher-bearers! – You feel sorry for them, do you?" He smacked at a mosquito on his neck. "So do I. They live on a planet with a constant temperate climate and no wildlife."

Otis laughed as she stepped back rapidly to cover the next batch of seats.

"And what are the women doing all this while?"

"Leading pampered lives, set upon gold-plated pedestals. Jealous, Captain?"

"No. Sounds boring."

"When Otis and I found ourselves in bad odour with the Government, Richards, we were given the choice of service in the Arctic or here. Sometimes we wonder if we made the right decision."

"I don't. If we were freezing in the Arctic we'd be longing for heat like this."

"She always stays disgustingly cool. Look, even Doctor Richards is getting red in the face."

"Not surprising," he said, rising from a slumped body. "It's purgatory in here. Hotter than hell."

"But all in a good cause, my boy. We can hide things much more efficiently in the jungle than we'd ever have managed in the Arctic."

"Can we talk so openly? Some of the team might be planted by the Powers."

"I've worked with this gang for a long time. Everybody's been sold down the Amazon like us."

"Or say they have," suggested Richards.

"We're vigilant. It's a small community. Everybody's involved but access to communication with officialdom outside is confined. Anyway, generally speaking, only newcomers are suspect. Like yourself."

Richards, colour already very high, flushed a deeper shade.

"But my father was an old friend of yours. How could…?"

"Most people come on recommendation. We have our network. But we're still vigilant."

Otis smiled at Richards.

"Take no notice, Doctor. Your new boss likes to aggravate."

Alban chuckled, mopping his brow and the back of his bulging neck.

Their tunics had darkened, perspiration spreading from their armpits the moment they had stepped into the furnace-heat of the craft. Though Otis appeared not so badly affected, she could feel sweat trickling down the hollow of her spine into her breeches.

"Why does this sector have so many space smashes?" asked Richards.

"An endless tract of jungle doesn't provide an easy way down."

"But that doesn't explain such a high number in trouble over this particular area in the first place." He stopped suddenly. "Do you lure them?"

"Lure them?"

"Like Cornishmen used to lure ships onto the rocks centuries ago?"

"The Powers deprive us of advanced technology. How could we manage that?" Alban smiled quizzically. "We'd need more than a few wreckers' lights on a headland, wouldn't we?"

Richards stared into his eyes.

"Yes. You would."

"Desperate times call for desperate measures," grated Otis.

"But how?"

"Your father's work on vector beams led to the system we use. Our rescued off-planet technicians provide the rest."

"Does my father know?"

"Yes."

Alban grasped Richards as if about to shake hands and they stood face to sweating face.

"It's necessary," he hissed. "We do everything we can for the casualties."

Richards swallowed and nodded.

Alban turned away.

"Here, bearers. Quickly!"

"We may have to be more sparing," said Otis. "If Doctor Richards feels suspicious, so might others."

They had reached the entrance to the forward cockpit, Otis still ahead.

"Not much chance for anyone in the nose-cone," said Alban wearily. "Would you like me to go first?"

"No."

She walked into the cabin.

"Yeugh!"

The foul reek was ten times worse than the stench pervading the rest of the vessel.

The pilot sprawled, head smashed against his bloodied controls. His co-pilot lay twisted in the other seat as if desperately trying to free his impossibly trapped legs.

Despite his bulk, Alban leapt to him in one movement. He removed the man's gloves, felt his pulse, touched cheeks and brow, examined his pupils.

"Why wear gauntlets in this heat?"

"I've no idea. He must have died only minutes before we arrived."

"Resuscitation?"

"No."

"So if he'd held on just a little longer…?"

The doctor nodded.

"Unlucky. Cause of death?"

"I'm not sure. Take a look, Richards. Could have been a massive heart attack, I suppose."

Doctor Richards moved round Otis to view the body from the front and drew in his breath sharply. "Nasty. His legs plus the shock of the impact?"

Alban shrugged.

Richards peered closer. "It may be heart failure. I think he died of fright."

"Terror at crashing to earth?" asked Otis.

"No. Something more immediate. He's holding this gun in a grip like a vice. Look at his face."

She stepped round the body and gazed upon the distorted features. Eyeballs rolled upward, the face had lips drawn back in a soundless scream revealing teeth already part of a dead man's skull. The ghastly mask of fear, combined with the tautly arched body, made Otis shiver. The sweat drenching her spine ran cold. She retreated quickly.

Meanwhile, Alban surveyed the cockpit. "I wonder if he thought the atmosphere outside was toxic and seeing this gash in the hull frightened him to death."

"Could that cause such terror?"

"Who knows? He's been firing this gun all over the place. Could have been hallucinating, I suppose."

"Perhaps he'd heard the ambulance or saw us coming and thought we were – well – somehow malevolent," said Richards.

"He wouldn't have seen us from here," said Otis, "nor heard anything. The bus is old but the engines are fine-tuned and run like a dream."

"Whatever, there's certainly nothing we can do for him now," sighed Alban.

"I'll arrange for a team to get started," said the captain.

"A ghastly shambles for the squad to clear up. Drinks all round in the mess tonight, I think," said Alban. "Let's get out. It's like living in hot soup."

He took a final look around the cockpit and shook his head.

Humming busily, a mass of insects moved darkly upon the head wound of the pilot.

"Damn heat. Damn jungle. Sometimes I wish I had chosen the Arctic."

A fly crawled across the cheek of the heart failure case. "Damn flies."

THRELL

The buzz. The swirl. The tingling pleasure.

Erica felt herself sinking into that helpless, happy frisson of delight.

"Is this the sort of feeling the drinkers of alcohol crave when they gather in the bars at the base of The Tiers?" she had asked Alexandrova as a child.

"I doubt it. This is more like sex. The more fulfilling sort, anyway."

Her tutor knew that Erica was too young to understand but later it would make sense.

"How could they give this up?"

"Some are not Threll anyway," Alexandrova had replied. "Others have limited talent and drink a little, too. They can travel the timelines to some extent but it's a haphazard pastime. They're mere dabblers. Even some of the highly talented cannot accept the responsibilities. Everyone must make their choice."

Now much older, Erica understood things better. Waking. Struggling to the surface. Arriving in an alien culture with potential enemies at every turn. The drinkers gave up the anxiety along with the ecstasy.

The bath water grew cool. She hauled herself upright. A towel hung on the rail close by and neatly folded over a chair were the clothes necessary for life in Three A.

"Threll?" asked Michael as Erica raised the fruit juice to her lips.

Life since her journey from the Vienna flat to London

had followed the usual routine. This was the first hint of danger.

She held the glass halfway to her lips and tilted her head slightly. "Sorry?"

It was the end of a beautiful friendship.

"Threll."

"What's that?" she asked. "Some kind of foreign toast? Like skol?"

"No," smiled Michael. "They're a group of people who don't drink alcohol."

"They're religious?"

"No. It disagrees with them, so I'm told. It was just a joke because you don't seem to drink."

"I do drink occasionally," she lied, smiling, "but could give it up very easily. Perhaps I'll join these... What are they called again?"

"Threll, but maybe they're a bit obscure. If you've not heard of them, I'll leave it at that."

His discomforted look should have been consolation but wasn't. Instead of getting on with the job, Erica had been indulging her sexual and emotional needs. No more.

After the concert the bar of the Royal Festival Hall, despite its open plan and a host of other patrons, had seemed quite intimate, for they'd both had eyes for nobody else. That was over now but the transition could not be too obvious.

"My friend's away tonight," sighed Erica. "I promised to get back fairly early to see to her cats. She allows me to stay when I'm in London so needs must. It's the nearest thing to paying rent."

He managed to look and sound disappointed which, after their very intimate clinches in a taxi the night before, hardly surprised her. She felt disappointed herself.

She rang Hector Graham from the Holland Park flat. Polly had no cats but was away. Every visit, Erica bought books from Hector, usually at book fairs. They always contained her instructions and details of pre-arranged hotel bookings so he must be trustworthy. The previous week, Michael had come and shaken Hector's hand and joined them as they sat chatting over a lunchtime snack.

"Nice chap. Not Threll," Hector said when he'd gone. "Not books either. Something to do with publicity for the Fair."

Hector sounded vague and puzzled on answering the phone. "Who?"

"Erica. Erica Gard. I bought books from you last week."

"Erica, of course. Sorry. Didn't expect to hear from you again for months."

"Who is this Michael Blackwood?"

"Oh, he got in touch? I gave him Polly's number. You seemed very interested and he's thoroughly smitten with you. I thought you travellers liked a good time when you were off-line. He's no problem, honestly."

"Maybe. But he knows something about the Threll."

"What!" Hector sounded appalled.

"Not much, perhaps, but the name."

"Hmm. Best give him the slip before you set off for York and Edinburgh."

Michael Blackwood might be ex-Threll, somebody who couldn't resist alcohol and got addicted, like poor Doreen in her squalid basement flat. Yet she enjoyed life and always made Erica welcome. Unlike Polly who, while saying the opposite, made her feel a nuisance.

Doreen, despite her shortcomings, was both likeable and discreet. Blackwood might be different. There were renegades, she'd heard, still retaining some power, snapped up by the opposition to root out genuine Threll. She feared the power of the other travellers. Some called them the Lerth, more or less the opposite to Threll. They wished to rule the time-lines for their own ends and remove all competition. Their emergence had put paid to the carefree, dilettante approach to life and travelling which the Threll had traditionally enjoyed.

Erica looked out onto the road from Polly's second floor window. Street lights were turning on and it had started to rain, making the pavements shine. She decided to leave the hire car parked beside the kerb and make her way to Doreen's, which was about midway between Earls Court and Gloucester Road stations. It might pre-empt being followed next morning.

After consulting the A to Z, Erica stuffed a sponge bag and underwear into her briefcase and grabbed her handbag. Walking through side turnings, she emerged onto Kensington High Street then plunged into the maze of roads on the other side. Heavy rain became visible, slanting beneath every street lamp. A horrible feeling crept over her. Somebody was following so she tried to put on speed. In her haste, she took an unintended detour into a cul-de-sac. A moment of panic gripped her. There was no escape. Erica turned around to find nobody there, in fact, nobody on the street at all. She would feel too exposed consulting the A to Z under a lamp so forced herself to concentrate on the route she had memorised. Nameplates at a street corner set her right but every step became painful. Her feet, like the rest of her, were soaked. The stupid court shoes she had to wear were cutting into her foot and making her heels sore.

Erica reached Doreen's with great relief, despite the water cascading down the area steps leading to her front door.

"Shall I make a sandwich for you for your journey?" asked Doreen, next morning, cigarette in mouth, fishing about on the cluttered kitchen top.

"No. I'll get something on the motorway."

"Rather you than me. You know the date, don't you?"

Erica frowned. "Yes, of course."

"Okay, you know your stuff. It's just I once forgot to check when I had to sign something. Didn't even know the year. Felt such a fool but managed to wriggle out of it."

"Nineteen ninety-eight."

"Right. Seems to be the farthest forward we can go so Michael calls it 'contemporary'." She yawned and stretched. "As you don't need anything, I needn't have got up at this unearthly hour."

It was eight thirty, not exactly the crack of dawn. According to Doreen, the car hire firm on the other side of the Cromwell Road didn't open till nine.

Erica laughed. "Go back to bed. Thanks for all your help and the travel bag and spare blouse and everything. I'll pop them in on my way back."

"No bother, Ricky. I'll always help you out. You just have to take me as you find me. Too much booze, too many late nights. You know."

And men and cigarettes, thought Erica.

"Any messages for anybody?" Doreen asked.

"None. You've not even seen me. I don't trust anyone at the moment except you."

But, in truth, she couldn't even be sure of Doreen.

Refusing the couple's offer of tea, Erica picked up the crumbling, leather-bound book. Turning brittle leaves, a smell of mouldy putrefaction arose which made her think of the Black Death. She tried not to breathe in.

There were two quite explicit references at the places which Hector had indicated in her written instructions and other less obvious passages. Clearly many Threll had lived in this timeline once and they'd not been that discreet. Presumably religion and a variety of superstitions had provided all the cover they needed.

Mr Walmer, with his ruddy face and thatch of white hair, looked entirely honest but certainly inflated the price he claimed to have been offered already. They haggled till Erica had a deal within Hector's guidelines and parted amicably.

Strolling through The Shambles in search of a celebratory coffee, she suddenly saw Michael Blackwood striding along the pedestrianised street. He was turning his head from side to side, scanning the throng of people.

Erica bolted into a shop. She watched him pass from behind a revolving stand of postcards showing the places in York there would now be no time to visit.

On the road, desperate for coffee, Erica made an early stop and phoned Jamie to tell him she was a day early.

"Forget Edinburgh," he said. "We've big trouble here. Lerth. You carry on to your next assignment and then get back to Vienna and Homeline."

"I've no other assignment."

"Then scat."

She rang Hector before returning to the car but there was no reply.

Making good time, Erica branched off the M1 for Coventry. She'd once, briefly, had a fling with an actor who worked there. Parking in a familiar spot near the theatre, she went and posted the book to Hector in its prepared postal bag, enclosing a note about her own and Jamie's problems. Back at the theatre café, Erica forced down a snack, too psyched-up to eat anything more substantial.

The rest of her journey proved uneventful. The London traffic no better or worse than usual, she returned the hire car to the Cromwell Road firm then went straight to Polly's. Special detours were out. Doreen would have to manage without the things she'd borrowed.

Dog-tired, the walk from Kensington High Street Station revived her a little. She didn't bother to go up to Polly's flat for her things. The other hire car from Heathrow, still parked outside, started first time.

There was no chance of an immediate flight, of course. More watchful than usual, Erica endured the familiar experience of hanging around in this timeline's airports: coffee, magazine, ladies' room for variety, newspaper, more coffee.

Much later, now arrived in Vienna, she took a cab to the Hotel Schoenbrunn and walked the two blocks to the flat.

Erica studied the unexceptional apartment building from across the way. All looked perfectly normal.

Spiralling downwards. A kind of sleep, echoing voices fading into dark silence. A struggle renewed, a clambering upwards, the buzz, the sensation of gratified flesh. The splash of water, the light.

The yellow smoothness of the bathroom wall and its distinctive perfume told Erica that this was her usual room in Central Hotel Special Block. Her own clothes were laid out in readiness. After shrugging into a bathrobe, she buzzed Services from the main room.

"I need a face-to-face debriefing."

"Hold, please," said the Duty Operator then, "Room 345 at nine in the morning. Supper will be sent to your room shortly. I hope you sleep well."

Fat chance, Erica thought, but she did.

"You've passed the test. Michael Blackwood reported you were brilliant," said Polly Struthers.

Her dislike of Polly made Erica suspect her of conniving with the Lerth. But here she was on Homeline and in a position of knowledge and power, so that couldn't be. To learn that the nervous energy she'd expended and the efforts made were just a test, a wild goose chase, added to her sense of resentment.

"Michael Blackwood's damn fussy when he's recruiting," said Polly. "I never dreamt you'd be successful."

Yes, the dislike is mutual, Erica thought.

"Not that I've any knowledge of his operation. My job is just liaison and supporting the network and the travellers passing through."

"I didn't think he could be Threll. Ex-Threll, perhaps. He drinks."

"That's easy to fake. In any case, it wouldn't matter within reason. He's moved to Three A permanently."

"Permanently!"

"Pretty drastic but we live in drastic times. Is it something you'd consider?"

"I don't know."

She thought of dramatic scenery, exciting capitals and beautiful cities like Salzburg. The Tiers overlooking the Great Lake were considered most wonderful but there was nothing on Homeline to compare with Earth's geographical diversity or the architecture of the old European cityscapes she'd seen. And Erica thought how her heart might race again with Michael as an ally.

"There are places and people I like but there's plenty that's horrible, too."

There was a buzz. Polly picked up the earpiece and listened.

"We'd like you to attend a further debrief in Room 903 in an hour. Okay?"

"You've always had such talent, Erica," said Alexandrova. "We need capable people like you to consolidate our position in Three A. Though your contacts aren't under immediate threat, life there is dangerous. We're at risk from these alien travellers in every timeline we reach. Some Threll who move permanently to Three A can travel back within that line and they're in the process of introducing our people onto computer records at the point where compilation began. Threll are living in Britain, America and many other places in the nineteen fifties, sixties and so on, paving the way. Much of the work is boring to Threll. Those who succeed best, fall in love, put down roots, start a family."

"Even Michael Blackwood?"

Alexandrova laughed. "He's not attached. He might be the perfect match for you, Erica, but he has a roving eye. But then so do you, I suspect. Michael has a more exciting job coordinating our activities and we're asking you to join his team."

"And to move there permanently?"

"Yes. How do you feel about your mother being left without family here?"

Erica shrugged. "Sad, but we don't have that much contact now."

Alexandrova sighed. "She once worked through Sao Paulo, you know. With your father working through Dallas, your family neatly covers the three routes into Three A. Your grandfather once travelled through Vienna, too, to monitor Asia and Africa. Nobody realised then that Three A would become so important."

"But why there, Alexandrova? Think of the discord. The Middle East, fragmenting cultural groups in Africa, Russia, the Balkans. Basques, Irish, Tamil Tigers, it's endless. And most with their own mad, bad bombers and assassins."

"Yes, there's boneheaded ideology, crime, corruption, disease, starvation but nowhere else do we have such advantage over our enemies. And for Threll it's a wealthy life. They can indulge themselves in many ways not possible here. Our population's increasing and merging all the time. Ultimately, Threll will outnumber the indigenous population and be a force for good."

"But that must be very long term."

"True but the process is in place and working. The Lerth mustn't be allowed to ruin it. See your mother and your friends before deciding. Should you go, I'm afraid you can only tell them you'll be away a long time. I'll need a decision very soon."

The outcome seemed inevitable. Sonya, her friend since childhood, had become totally obsessed with her new baby and spoke non-stop of nothing else. Erica was pleased to get away.

The remnants of a gang of other friends still met in a bar in the basement of The Tiers. Many had gone their separate ways but Yuri, a man she had once lusted after, still held court. His stunning looks no longer attracted her. His life seemed shallow. The whole group drank, laughed a lot, and appeared to enjoy life, yet to Erica it seemed a waste of time and talent. Her call of "See you soon" as she left sounded sincere but wasn't.

Her mother, like most people with Threll power, had a comfortable, above average lifestyle. Her apartment was halfway up The Tiers with fine views over the Lake. When Erica entered, Josephine Gard sat at her keyboard playing a melodic nocturne with her usual flair and tenderness. The door to the balcony stood open and the curtains fluttered in the breeze. It was how Erica always remembered her.

"Come and sit down," her mother called, patting the

space beside her on the music stool with one hand while sustaining a series of chords with the other.

She brought the piece to a close with a low melancholy note, raised her hands from the keyboard and turned to her daughter.

"Such a long time."

"Yes. Sorry. I'm travelling more than ever now."

"Oh dear. Presumably you're going to disappear like your father."

"I thought he was coming back."

"Perhaps. More likely, he's enjoying the company of a variety of people in Texas much too much to ever return here."

"I might be away for quite a long time, myself."

Sharing the stool as if it were a loveseat, Erica sat with her back to the keyboard. Their eyes met.

"I see," whispered her mother.

"Come in, Ricky!" said Doreen. "Oh! Brought your luggage, then."

"Yes. Polly tries very hard but we really don't like each other. Can I stay till I've got my own place sorted out?"

"Of course. Nobody likes Polly much but we treat her nice, seeing she's our link with Homeline. What did you tell her?"

"Nothing. I need to get myself organized to go out again very shortly to meet Michael for dinner. Thought I'd phone her later with explanations and excuses."

"Lucky old you. Dinner with dishy Mikey."

"You know him well?"

"Of course. He's my boss and now yours. You must be pretty good. He's a fussy devil. Has to be. You'll get your briefing tonight and before long you'll be doing the beguiling; finding talented Threll males and using all your charms to make them give up Homeline for Hell on Earth."

"Is it that bad?"

"No! You know my way of talking, Ricky. I love it."

"Is that what I'll have to do? Chat up males?"

"Just part of the job, not all."

"Sounds like prostitution to me."

"No, nothing like. You'll be doing it for ethical reasons and you'll enjoy it. I've got to go out, too. I'd better get myself organized. Make yourself at home."

Doreen sang at the top of her voice in the bathroom. She left about ten minutes ahead of Erica, calling, "Ciao!"

The tube platform at Gloucester Road was crowded. She glimpsed Doreen at the far end, still waiting, and began to work her way through the throng towards her. Feeling the draught of an oncoming train, Erica stopped to look again. Doreen was moving towards the front of the platform. Suddenly, Polly appeared behind her, hand poised at the small of her back. The train could be heard clearly and Erica watched appalled, immobile, then managed to shout, "Doreen! Look out!"

Doreen sprang back from the brink and disappeared into the crowd as the train thundered out of its black hole and began to decelerate beside the platform.

Polly came stamping up.

"You damn fool, Erica! She's Lerth. A whole pack has been uncovered and they've got to be dealt with. Even Michael Blackwood."

"Not Doreen. Michael, perhaps, but not Doreen."

"Yes, you idiot. Doreen. No wonder Michael selected you. He can pull the wool over your eyes. He's choosing people in the interests of the Lerth. Come back to the flat and we'll draw up a plan of campaign."

The tube train gave off an electrical hum.

"I've got an assignment that can't wait," Erica replied, listening for the sliding doors.

"What can be more important than…?"

They were closing. She pushed Polly away and leapt in. The doors shut, started to open again then, to her relief, slammed to. Polly stepped up and glared through the glass. Erica stared back and, after an initial jerk, the train glided away. Soon, heart beating fast, she gazed at her own deathly pale face among the crowd, reflected against the blackness of the tunnel and the waving lines of cable.

Michael rose and kissed her in greeting, holding her close.

They had a view of the Thames from a window table in the upstairs restaurant of the Festival Hall. She would have found the lights rippling on the water and the London skyline idyllic except her mind was in turmoil.

"Soon, we'll be able to go back and see this site before these buildings were here. You have great talent, Erica. It's a privilege to have you with us. I knew you were brilliant the moment I mentioned the Threll to you. Do you remember?"

"Yes. My heart sank."

He laughed. "Drink halfway to your lips, you said 'Threll? What's that? Some kind of toast like skol?' I thought, something's gone wrong. This isn't the right girl. She knows nothing of the Threll."

Erica didn't necessarily believe him. Michael had to be a good actor to do his job. But could he also be a supporter of the Lerth? Staring at him, thinking of her last conversation with Alexandrova, she asked, "Can we really move backwards in this timeline?"

"Oh, yes. We always go in pairs."

"Share the bath?" asked Erica, somewhat appalled.

"No. A shower. That's why there must be genuine feeling between us as well as talent. We clasp each other and fly. You'll like visiting the London of the past. Our work's important but we can enjoy ourselves, too."

Erica picked at her food only half listening as he talked of the Festival of Britain from which the Hall derived its name. Michael enjoyed life, which seemed genuine Threll, whereas Polly had no *joie de vivre*. If told of her accusation he'd say Polly supported the Lerth and he and Doreen didn't. Erica wanted it to be that way round but perhaps life never turned out like that.

Inwardly she sighed. Working with Polly would be impossible so, traitor or no, cooperating with Michael and Doreen seemed the only way.

"She's a bit suspect at the moment. How are you getting on with her?"

Erica had missed the beginning. "Who? Doreen?"

"No. Polly."

"Oh. Because we don't hit it off, I suspected her of being Lerth but she's high in the Echelon on Homeline." Erica decided to take the plunge. "She suggested that you and Doreen were colluding with the Lerth."

Michael sat up very straight. "That's very incriminating. When?"

"On my way here. She was going to push Doreen under a train."

"What!"

Erica told all. "I suppose you'll say she's Lerth and you and Doreen aren't."

"Of course."

Alexandrova, who always stressed her talents, became her anchor now. By contrast, Polly belittled them. All her instincts told Erica that Doreen was genuine. Polly was right, though. Michael could take her in because of her feelings for him.

"I'm Threll, Erica, and need your support. We've got to protect Hector now and quickly." He called for the bill and asked directions to the nearest phone. "You ring Hector. I'll settle up. Tell him our suspicions about Polly are correct. If she rings asking to meet him, he's to say 'yes' but not to go."

Hector answered after one ring. "Erica. I thought it would be Michael."

"He asked me to phone and warn you about Polly."

"She's already rung and said we must meet urgently. I've said we could meet down on the platform at Camden Town Station."

"Don't go Hector. It's a trap."

"I know. Doreen's already phoned. But somebody should go."

"Hold on. Michael's coming."

Michael listened then said, "Southbound platform? Right. It's back to Homeline for you, Hector. Clear everything in your study that needs clearing and kiss your wife good-bye. Sorry. We'll pick you up in a taxi in about an hour on Heath Street near Hampstead Station. Okay?"

"Not okay," growled Michael, dialling again. "He'll miss his wife and she won't even know where he's gone or why. One of those men who slip out for cigarettes one day and disappear from the face of the earth."

"I didn't know he had a wife. She's never answered the phone."

"No. There's a separate line in his study."

"But he'll be back, surely."

"No. He's too vulnerable. We can hide in the past and change our names and addresses and adjust our bank accounts before we return but Hector's position makes him a sitting duck. Besides, he has to warn Homeline about Polly and arrange for new contacts for us. It'll be a while before they're fully operational. Damn Polly. What's the attraction of the other side?"

"None of us like her much. Maybe they said they did."

"Threats are more probable." He'd got through. "Harry? The situation with Polly is definite. Try and apprehend her at Camden Town Station." He relayed the relevant details. "I suggest two by taxi and two by tube from Mile End. Did Doreen and Roger get off? Good. Tell her to rendezvous with Michael and Erica, Kensington, sixty-three, when she's back. She's at risk and not to operate contemporary. You should be okay your end but stay vigilant. Cheers."

Hector had no luggage, simply a large briefcase and a long face. Nothing could console him.

At the house in Fulham where they dropped him, Erica was introduced to a woman named Kathy.

"Get somebody onto checking out Polly's flat," Michael told her. "It's probably an outlet for Lerth travelling here. Keep it tied."

Erica gasped, "I stayed there quite often."

"Did you leave belongings there?"

"No. I've moved in with Doreen."

"Oh and keep an external watch on Doreen's. Got the resources?"

Kathy nodded. "And two minders for Hector. All the way to Vienna."

Michael hugged Hector. "We're sorry to lose you."

"Can't you tell Irene, give her a hint?"

Michael shook his head. "Sorry. You know how it is."

The taxi took them on to a house in Kensington. Michael hustled her inside.

"We've no time to lose. You have to fly, Erica, but with the minimum amount of instruction. Your ability will get you through. Nineteen sixty-three is a year we find easy to access, that's why I've chosen it for our rendezvous with Doreen. The shower's upstairs. I'll show you the rest of the house when we arrive."

The large shower room contained two wooden chairs,

one set each side of a wide cubicle. The semi-transparent sliding doors stood open revealing shiny yellow tiles, reminiscent of Homeline. Beside each chair was an empty towel rail.

"We must each have a towel the same colour," said Michael, taking a pair of orange bath towels from an airing cupboard and throwing one to Erica. She hung it neatly on her rail.

"Strip off and leave your clothes folded over the chair."

She obeyed. Michael did the same. It was like preparing for timeline travel, nothing very erotic about it, but once they stood inside the cubicle with the doors closed, he wrapped his arms about her.

"Relax," he said. "Think of nineteen sixty-three in any way that you can imagine and use whatever technique you normally employ when crossing the timelines."

The instruction seemed impossible. She had no conception of the year except to go back a long way then stop. And crossing timelines just came naturally. Erica had never analysed how she did it.

Eyes shut, clasped together, water cascading, cold, warm, hot. Eyes open to sunshine then light fading, wet skin surfaces sliding against each other, heat spreading, torsos undulating, glowing, fiery. A smell of musk and they were spinning, flying. Arms and legs spread wide both joined together at fingertips and toes. Their mouths wide open in effort, ecstasy, fear, fear of losing the other. A coming together, bodies wrapped tight, a slow spin, the running down of the roundabout, moist warmth, darkness, breathlessness, the chuckle of water. Silence.

The towels were white, the clothing different.

"Excellent," said Michael. "We've gone back and we're safe." He held up the trousers on his chair. "Might be sixty-three. We'll check later. I'll show you the bedroom before we get dressed. That's if you're in a bedroom kind of mood."

Erica was. Preparing to travel had been mundane, asexual but travelling itself had left her feeling lustful and passionate.

"The train robbery story has just broken." Michael laid down the newspaper. "Eighth of August, sixty-three. I wonder if Doreen and Roger will be as accurate."

Erica had expected to meet Doreen immediately but Michael said it could be weeks, even months, before they got together. "It's not an exact science. She'd aim for mid-year, end of June, beginning of July. We've managed early August but she could have landed in September or October. Of course, if Doreen's arrived before us we may see her within a few days. We'll frequent mutual haunts. There are regular pubs and cafés we visit. We become a part of the barfly crowd. You'll learn a lot that way. We don't drink much alcohol, of course. You needn't drink at all. That, at least, is easier for a woman."

Kensington hadn't altered much. Ground level shopfronts and names were different but most of the architecture above remained the same. In Derry and Toms, Barkers and a variety of other stores she rapidly learnt to cope with the crazy currency, silly prices and current fashion. Afterwards Erica would walk back to the exquisite little Georgian house, one of a row, just off the High Street.

Lunchtimes and early evenings, she and Michael often drank in a variety of pubs along the High Street ranging from the Goat at one end to the Holland Arms at the other. Erica enjoyed the company of the barflies of both sexes and learnt a lot about current ideas, slang and usage as well as popular topics of conversation, including sex which was often on their agenda when they returned to the house. Though enjoyable and leisurely, it seemed like life in a vacuum.

The television in the living room showed boring programmes on a small monochrome screen. Erica tried to watch sometimes because the barflies often talked about TV shows but she preferred seeing films at the Odeon. Afterwards, they often went to Dino's, close by Earls Court Station, and drank cappuccinos at one of the Formica-top tables.

They had plenty of time to talk.

"I once met your father."

"Did you? I haven't seen him since I was a child."

"No. That's sad. He runs our entire North American project. It's very complex. He's a brilliant man, the one who discovered that we could travel back within this line. Of course, eventually he learnt that it diminished the ability to jump the timelines but it was too late for him by then. Maybe you'll get to meet him now you're here permanently."

One day he said, "I've got to leave for seventy-six and various other years to sort out new names, flats and so on for you, Doreen and myself. Any particular name you fancy?"

"Doreen calls me Ricky."

"Richards sounds a good surname. First name?"

"How about my mother's? Josephine."

"Josephine Richards. Excellent. I'm leaving this afternoon."

"From the shower room?"

"Not this one. Another property in South London."

Erica spent a discontented evening watching television and riffling through magazines. Michael would be gone ages and, worse, going through the shower with some other woman and, no doubt, falling into bed with her in nineteen seventy-six.

To her surprise and delight he walked through the door next morning.

"You didn't go then?"

"Yes. I spent a fortnight in seventy-six. Wonderful weather. They were having a heatwave. Then three days in eighty-nine and a week in ninety-eight. The return was incredibly accurate. We got back last night."

"Who did you travel with?"

"It's better I don't say."

About three weeks later, Doreen walked into Dino's and did a convincing double-take on seeing them. "Mike! Ricky! Long time no see."

She sat down and, twirling spaghetti and drinking cappuccino, updated them on the news of what she called Contemp.

"Hector got back safely. We've got one temporary go-between, an American called Chuck, very dishy." She made a sexy growling noise in her throat. "When we're all back to normal he's going to fly over from Texas to see us."

"Any news of Polly?"

"They tried to pick her up at Camden Town but no joy."

"Pity. She'll go to ground. We've got to go back to Contemp ourselves soon to hold the line, so take care. We're all Londoners, incidentally, with new names, flats and bank accounts and Threlldom owns even more property in London."

"Getting in on the ground floor, again, eh?" grinned Doreen.

"Erica!"

She ignored the call and continued down to the Piccadilly Line platform. Her name was Josephine now. No doubt, her adaptability was being tested.

Somebody grabbed her arm. "It is you, Erica!"

She turned to find Polly staring at her, white-faced with fury. "You traitor! You've become a tool of the Lerth!"

Erica's heart sank as, feeling a draught on her cheek, Polly forced her towards the platform's edge.

"Don't! Talk! We need to talk."

Hearing the rumble of the train, Erica found extra strength and dug in her heels. They both rotated. She swung Polly around and let go, intending to run. With a long-drawn-out scream Polly teetered over the edge. The train roared out of the tunnel. Erica couldn't look, couldn't contemplate what had happened and rushed through the nearest gap in the platform. Running upstairs, she found her feet clanging on metal. The emergency stairs spiralled upward. Erica stopped to listen and rest her aching legs. There were only muffled echoes. At the top, she opened a door and emerged onto the concourse near the ladies' toilets.

"I want to return to Homeline."

"You're in the clear, you know."

He handed her the previous night's Standard.

Headed, 'TUBE DEATH', the article said an inquest concluded that Polly Struthers, a senior bank employee, had taken her own life while the balance of her mind was disturbed: "No family has been traced and a woman who called out and tried to stop her has not come forward. Colleagues were unaware that Miss Struthers had any problems."

"I still want to return."

Polly's words about conspiring with the Lerth had sown further seeds of doubt in her mind.

"It's probably too late. In Vienna you may find the locks changed on the flat. The housekeeper will tell you there's been a lot of refurbishment and give you a new key but inside will be only a shower, no bath. We've all had doubts, Josephine, but ultimately we're glad we stayed." He took her hand. "They call it Earth as if nobody else had such a substance to walk on. We're going to colonise Earth, Jo, you and I. There will be others, millions, but we're the forerunners. Will you toast our future success in wine?"

She gazed at the view of the Thames, paths of shimmering silver light converging on their window table. Looking around the restaurant, imbibing the atmosphere, the sense of time and place, she knew she'd become a Londoner. There was no going back.

"Yes, I'll drink a toast in alcohol. To the Threll."

"Threll?" asked Josephine Richards.

He looked askance. "What's that, Esperanto?"

To her relief, Paul Eliot looked like making the grade. Fussy about who might be clasped to her bosom travelling the line, his attractive looks and personality counted for a lot. Some of the previous ones, though better looking, had been as transparent as glass.

"They're an unusual group who don't drink. I just wondered."

"I never drink and drive," he smiled. "Maybe I should join."

His excuses for leaving early were excellently plausible. Paul asked if he might drop her anywhere.

"No, thanks all the same. I'll perhaps see you again sometime."

She smiled in satisfaction as he hurried away.

INFORMATION FROM A PHILHARMONIC SPY

Today my heart raced when I thought Joseph Haydn had caught me out as a spy.

When I asked for details of the winter festival called Christmas, Joseph eyed me with great suspicion. At last, he smiled and clapped me on the shoulder.

"You and your jokes," he said. "Make the most of the festivities, for once they are over we must travel to Esterhaza Palace."

He is a kind and generous man. If all humankind were like him we would have no fears. His music is the only thing that gives me comfort in this appalling place.

I dread the journey. As we suspected, they rely on harnessing other creatures to till the soil, transport goods and move from place to place. Exquisitely ornate carriages are made for men of means. They are smoothed, painted and polished by squads of skilled and highly trained operatives and others clean and rub the draught animals until they shine. Everything is show and in vain. Once embarked upon the rutted ways a vehicle either becomes bogged down in mud or covered in dust according to the weather. Inevitably, too much rain falls or not enough, never the happy medium.

We arrived in Eisenstadt in a drenching, terrifying thunderstorm that also made my heart thump. I am still not used to this clumsy body which puts me at further risk.

Conditions are better here but my chamber has a stone

floor and an icy draught. The oubliette in the part of the building in which I dwell, and where I must suffer freezing blasts and inhale the most noxious stench, would astonish and horrify you. Furthermore, my heels and toes are red and raw from the cold and itch unbearably. To scratch them causes the most excruciating pain.

Another discomfort is caused by the ridiculous wig I needs must wear which is infested with small biting creatures. I cannot catch them and the powder smothering the head coverings causes a rash upon my neck and makes me sniffle and sneeze.

Nothing useful of current politics can be divined in this household. I am cold, ill, sore and bitten by parasites and ask permission to give up the assignment and return to the perfumes of home and the meeting of minds in a comfortable temperature. The stressful noises of this world make the thought of returning to the silence of the kin all the more appealing.

It is almost impossible for me to explain music but, as you insist, I shall try.

Joseph Haydn is the director of the Prince's orchestra. He is a kind of computer programmer, producing on paper a series of dots, lines and squiggles which instruct the players which frequencies to produce and at what rate. Different notes are produced on diverse instruments by varying the air vibrations within, a fascinating use of simple science. Even more compelling is the way the programmer makes the sounds blend, run, slow, halt, race again and intertwine.

I have heard Bach and Mozart as well as Joseph's own programs and marvel at the flowing melodies running up and down the scale and the fiddle bows moving in unison, with every player making his contribution. The whole operation calls for ingenuity, foresight, planning and a great deal of cooperation. People work together to produce beauty. Perhaps, after all, there are the makings of a peaceful planet.

The Palace of Esterhaza, though primitive by our standards, affords the most civilised accommodation I have enjoyed so far. Unfortunately, it is in the wilds of Hungary in the middle of a swamp.

Prince Nikolaus prefers to live here to anywhere else. Joseph complains of the isolation but admits that as a result he writes more music. His fame has spread to many lands regarding program-making, which they call composing.

Music is the only thing which makes life endurable, giving brief respite from the thousand pinpricks which are part of life on Earth.

When I said as much to a fiddle player in the orchestra he said it was sex which did that for him. This activity is totally beyond my ken and I may have said something which compromises my position. I live in constant fear of discovery.

I seem to have little access to useful political information at Esterhaz. However, I learn of rumours of revolution fermenting in France.

It is unlikely to come to fruition. The ruling class holds absolute sway by keeping the rest in ignorance and poverty. Lack of education and material resources ensures that those of lower status have no opportunity to nurture a leader strong enough to endure.

Meanwhile, because I am a servant in a rich man's house my living conditions are good by local standards. My clothes are of the softest and smoothest available and yet they chafe my skin in a dozen delicate places and nothing relieves the soreness.

Wine, like music, offers some relief but can have devastating effects. A wonderful release of tension builds to euphoria and finally loosens all control over the tongue. My fellows laugh at my babblings and say if I talk like a madman about my lunatic relatives I shall end up in the asylum. I dare not ask what this is but I know it cannot be good.

Oh, how I hate this world. I am at great risk yet achieving nothing. I implore you to let me return.

Goose grease is my latest salvation. It reeks abominably and is no cure but relieves for a time the soreness of my human crevices and also helps the itching of my toes and heels, an affliction known as chilblains, I learn, and common in winter.

Spring beckons with the promise of some let-up from the stink of medication.

A kitchen wench keeps making advances to me to the amusement of the other servants. They make strange remarks about what I should do. Their advice frightens me. I am so ignorant and cannot even ask dear, kind Joseph. An adult male is meant to know and I am about to be exposed.

My immediate return would make excellent sense. There is nothing political to report and never will be.

The summer has been insufferably hot, stench-filled and unhygienic.

There is revolution in France, we hear, death and disorder in Paris.

At Esterhaz there are also changes. Since Prince Nikolaus' death, little interest has been shown in music. Joseph plans to go to London, making me fearful for his safety. By this world's standards old and not robust, he must make a jolting, dangerous journey across a strife-torn continent then embark upon the ghastly sea. To propel their watercraft, they rely upon the force of the wind which, like the rain, is always too much or too little.

In answer to your further questions, music does nothing truly practical but soothes and relaxes. Unless you heard you would never understand.

Your instructions will be followed to the letter. I shall be glad to leave. I have had successful and pleasurable liaison with the kitchen maid and, as a result, am in deep trouble. I cannot tell why. She is about to reproduce, which I thought was the intention.

Once over the French border I shall transfer to another being. I am sick of being a servant at everyone's beck and call. Perhaps I shall find a more exalted host whose position of power will further our knowledge.

My days as an aristocrat were short-lived. Further transfer had to be speedy.

Now I am the lowest of the low, yet the mystifying undercurrents in this city still put me in danger. Not only through my ignorance but also because of my sex. I cannot adequately describe the humiliation of being female. People are aggressive because you are small and wear skirts. They touch you and make crude suggestions and sometimes actually try to follow them up. A blow with a clenched fist has proved very effective but I also keep a sharp knife in my knitting bag.

The horrors of Paris are impossible to describe. Suffice

to say, decapitations and gore feature prominently.

My living quarters are cupboard-sized, sparse and malodorous. It is difficult to keep myself clean because, as usual on this accursed world, the plumbing is not poor but non-existent.

I am trapped in disgusting penury. To be anything other than poor leads to the guillotine. For kinship's sake allow me back to sanity, safety and cleanliness.

Relief fills me at being male again. I have become a soldier and can walk in comparative safety wearing my white breeches and blue tunic jacket.

Soon order will be restored with the King, Assembly and Constitution in place supported by the Army. Only the other night, sitting in a café with a fellow officer, an affray erupted in the street. My companion, named Bonaparte, and only a little fellow, went outside and the whole pack of revolutionaries fled.

"My friend, you are a brave man," I said, joining him on the now peaceful boulevard.

"Brave? No," he replied. "To be assertive and to expect others to obey is my nature. Would it were the King's. As things stand, we may lose everything."

"You think so?"

"But yes. The king is as weak as water. You would not catch me wearing a cap of liberty, reciting and singing every word as instructed if revolutionaries had entered my palace."

Not that he has a palace, you understand, or ever will.

Bonaparte maintains that the enemies surrounding "poor France" are waiting for the demise of the King before pouncing. He spoke of England where Joseph resides at present. I would love to see his kind face again, though he would never recognise me. I might go and learn something of their politics but am deterred by the thought of crossing the ocean in one of the death traps they call ships.

A cold wind blows on this strange shore and I have been exceedingly ill. The motion of the sea has the most appalling effect.

The English are a puzzling race. They treat me like an imbecile simply because I come from a different part of their planet. The sooner a suitable English host can be found the better.

The inn at Dover affords a good fire in the public room but my bed-chamber freezes the blood.

Now that I am well settled in my new host, England does not seem so bad. My business in the City of London is importing tea, spices and other commodities. English wine is undrinkable but there are other beverages, ale and a Scottish drink called whisky.

Haydn is still in London. Many public concerts are held. Beethoven's wonderful Third Symphony was played the evening before last and sure encompasses everything you need to know about this planet.

He dedicated the work to Napoleon, the very same Bonaparte that I knew in Paris. Beethoven believed that thanks to him there might be true democracy with, indeed, liberty, fraternity and equality. When Napoleon made himself Emperor he dashed the hopes of Beethoven and many more besides. The composer tore up the title page of his work and the symphony is now known as the Eroica.

Defensive towers are being built around the coast for fear of Bonaparte. Children are told that if they are not good "Old Boney" will get them. His invincibility makes invasion almost certain.

That you wish to hear more of politics and nothing of music is quite understood. However, I mentioned the Eroica simply because of its relevance to the political situation.

Now well established, it seems worthwhile to remain in England, therefore I turn down your option to return.

Thanks to my import business, good French wines as well as brandy, Madeira, port and sherry are readily available to me and, of course, I can afford concert subscriptions.

Despite the sea victory at Trafalgar, the British are unlikely to succeed again the might of Napoleon on land. Their army would have the disadvantage of having to transport itself across the Channel. They cannot arrive other than in disarray and exceedingly sick.

I comprehend your concern but return would be premature. Waterloo has paved the way for a peaceful world and there will be no more war.

My handsome new servant, Clara, thinks of nothing but love and peace. She accompanies me to concerts dressed as the proper lady. I may even marry her, for the physical side of life proves to be pure pleasure and not the problem I envisaged. We heard Beethoven's Sixth Symphony this week which is full of contrast and joyful melody.

Incidentally, my firm now deal in another excellent drink called gin.

Although a lot of catching up is needful in regard to

technology, there are the makings here of an idyllic life and this might be the perfect planet.

Your ultimatum appals me. However, if the choice is between returning and remaining to explore the Americas then the journey to the New World shall be undertaken though not without trepidation. My stomach quakes at the thought of crossing the ocean again. If only I could skim above the waves in a warm, indestructible travel-pod.

Joseph Haydn died in Vienna during the French occupation. A sad loss. I shall never forget him. I believe his music will be remembered forever.

As to the New World, the nightmare of the crossing seemed to go on forever. Below decks, dim and stinking, people were packed like cargo with barely elbow room.

Food and fresh water should have been provided daily by the captain but the man was a charlatan and kept everyone pitifully short of rations.

We often encountered freezing cold mists. Any sudden drop in temperature sent the sailors scurrying to the rails to peer anxiously ahead for icebergs.

After six weeks at sea a passenger caught ship's fever and died. The dread disease spread like wildfire in the overcrowded steerage.

Although painful and often alarming to change hosts too frequently, I did so three times during that perilous voyage, finishing up as an incredibly robust and healthy female named Jane. Truly a survivor, she does not succumb to sea-sickness and is unaffected by vomit or the smell of urine.

We stepped onto *terra firma* this morning to begin the journey inland. Though, doubtless, nothing other than uncomfortable, I shall feel a good deal safer than travelling on water.

My new profession ensures travel all over the Continent. As the wilderness is explored and developed so we shall follow to the new townships.

I am a shapely young female which, for once, seems an advantage. Gentlemen are helpful, offering to carry luggage and assist in many little chores.

Dancing seems to be a natural talent with me and the lively music and the atmosphere in the bars where we perform are exhilarating. At present we are in Cincinnati and I have a wonderful beau who meets me after my stint in the saloon.

The whole country is a surprise. Expecting log cabins and the necessity to live rough, instead we find all the larger settlements have brick buildings. There are hotels, shops and sidewalks.

Only a few Indians and fur trappers live in the wilderness but Robert says soon there will be a whole new civilisation there with agriculture, livestock and great townships.

Our company is heading west to St Louis tomorrow with a variety of stops on the way. Then we go south to Memphis on the great Mississippi. To my joy, Robert says he will be coming too.

I have learned that Robert's money comes from gambling on the river boats. This entails playing games of chance for monetary units. He is less than honest for I have observed him using sleight of hand. Yet the strangers taking part seem so obsessed with their own efforts to gain something for nothing that they either ignore his methods or are completely oblivious to them. This was a depressing enough discovery but worse followed.

Here in the South are great plantations. The owners are

white-skinned and live in splendid houses. The plantation workers are a different, darker race.

"Robert, these workers seem to live in such poor conditions," I said one day. "How much are they paid?"

"Paid?" he replied and laughed. "You really are an ignorant girl. Everybody knows they're paid nothing. They're slaves."

This continent seemed so exciting with its opportunity for a fresh start, like a colony on a new and promising planet. That there would be a worm within the bud was, perhaps, inevitable. Earth does nothing but thwart the idealistic.

Despite missing the beverages, the music and the physical contact, to leave seems the only sensible course. I look forward to the well-ordered, perfumed cleanliness and the silent communication of home.

That you opposed my return turned out for the best. The current dispute has escalated into civil war. The opposing sides are often termed the North and the South. The North wants the South to become part of its Union of States but the Southern States will not give up their independence and have formed a loose Confederation of their own. Money and trade are at the heart of the dispute but also the abhorrent slavery, which the North opposes. The South cannot afford to give up the cheap labour of the slave trade even if it wanted.

Being domiciled in the South, the future looks bleak for me. The Confederate Army has had much success in battle under the brilliant General "Stonewall" Jackson. Apparently a very noble person with a reputation for kindness to negroes, he is, unfortunately, fighting with huge success on the wrong side. Insinuating myself close enough, some untoward accident could, perhaps, be engineered on his behalf.

For me to kill is forbidden and to maim or injure a crime. You may sit in judgment and deplore my intent but you cannot understand how embroiled one becomes being on the surface of this planet. In any case, such an action would be in our own best interests. The kin surely do not want the faction which subjugates and enslaves other races to succeed.

Whatever happens, I shall ultimately head north as my sole desire is to be with the Unionist Army even though they are about to be defeated.

I am well aware of the wilful iniquity of my ways. To interfere in the outcome of events on a planet under observation remains a heinous crime and never works to our advantage in the long run.

In the short term, my ruse worked. As the sentry on duty, I pretended to believe that Jackson and his companions were Unionists as they returned to camp after dark. My shot, aimed to wound, not to kill, and in that respect proved successful. But the General's arm had to be amputated, a sickening and sordid business like all supposed healthcare is on this world. As a result, he developed pneumonia and died. Please realise, his death was not intentional. There will be trouble enough for me without that.

The South is in disarray. Shortly there will be victory for the North and an end to slavery. Thankfully, the negroes will achieve equality and no longer be poor, downtrodden and reviled. At last they will receive as good an education as the whites and responsible, well-paid jobs will be open to them.

Some progress is being made. In Kansas City I used a water closet, a wonderful development towards hygiene.

My relationships with individual human beings continue to be close and physically satisfying. However, my mental attitudes are quite alien and can trigger off disputes.

For example, just recently Adam Collins and I had a close and loving relationship. He bought me presents: flowers, perfume, all kinds of fripperies.

One day he burst in upon me waving some pieces of pasteboard in a state of happy excitement.

"Look, Theodora! The Wild West Show's in town and I've got some tickets."

"Wild West Show! What's that?"

"Why, Dora, it's the best show ever, run by Buffalo Bill. You must've heard of him!"

"The name's kind of familiar but…"

"Well Buffalo Bill's a nickname. His real name's Colonel William Cody. He helped open up this country, working for the Pony Express while he was still a kid, well awful young, sixteen maybe. Riding seventy-five miles a day across the wilderness through storm, wind or baking sun turns a boy into a man, that's for sure. Then as a scout with the United States Army he fought in the campaigns again the Sioux and the Cheyenne. With his experience of the plains, Cody knew the ways of the Indians."

"And did many Indians get hurt?"

"Oh sure. Hundreds, maybe thousands died."

"And why Buffalo Bill?"

"That's from when he was killing buffalo."

"What?" I said, aghast. "Why, Adam?"

"The Colonel had a contract, see, to supply the railroad with fresh buffalo meat. They were building the Kansas Pacific then, pushing their way west. Those guys had a tough job and they sure needed to eat. The story goes that Bill Cody killed four thousand eight hundred buffalo in eighteen months and one time he killed sixty-nine in a day. What a man, huh? You'll just love his show."

Wild horses could not have dragged me to the Wild West Show. To Adam and his fellow humans Buffalo Bill is a hero. The kin would consider him the worst type of criminal; one who had made a major contribution to obliterating a species and causing the decline of the Red Indian tribes which had inhabited this continent long before white races began to colonise it.

When Adam finally believed that I would not go with him to the show, a most bitter quarrel ensured.

Now approaching Topeka, travelling alone, the railroad which all those dead buffalo helped to build clatters rhythmically beneath me.

An aimless wanderer, I learn of a way of life but nothing seems relevant. As male, female, little makes sense. Being an engineer, lawyer's wife, cowhand or, most unpleasant of all, horse, offered no enlightenment.

You may think this world small from your great distance but its vastness seems unending when you are alone, crawling over its surface by slow and primitive transport.

Crisscrossing the land to no good purpose, I've been to Wichita, Oklahoma City and Tulsa; to Abilene, Amarillo, Albuquerque; Phoenix, Fresno and Reno; Cheyenne, Champaign, Chicago and here I've come to a halt.

Chicago is cold. Discomfort follows me along the purposeless streets. Giving up the human pleasures accounts for some of my depression. It would be so easy to consume alcohol or copulate or both but until these physical desires are stifled, I know my other longing to return home cannot be gratified.

Tall buildings dominate the city. Without any of the technology which we possess these beings are producing great feats of engineering. There my admiration ends. The stockyards and slaughterhouses of Chicago would both astound and disgust you. Although I have eaten flesh regularly for over a century, using animal products made sense with the limited resources available.

Now there is no limitation. Animals are reared on a vast scale and brought to Chicago to be sold or slaughtered. The yards cover a huge area, the space of another city again. Death is dealt out routinely and the sight of such butchery sickens me.

My duties on Earth have been long-drawn-out and largely uncomfortable. Nothing can be gained now on behalf of the kin. My visit must be deemed an expensive failure and any punishment due, I accept for the sake of experiencing again the silence and hygiene of home with its warm, sweet-smelling surroundings.

Once more I have to accept your decision and remain on this accursed world.

Back in New York, I find the city has spread outwards and upwards. In a deep crevasse between tall buildings of concrete and glass, I saw and recognised a concert hall with a well-dressed gentleman about to enter. With a supreme effort, my spirit was transferred. So, entering the Music Hall on Seventh Avenue, by great good fortune, we heard the first performance of Dvorak's symphony "From the New World"! The second movement is a melodic and heart-rending lullaby, the other movements tuneful and exciting. Some passages even evoked nostalgia for the wide open spaces so happily left behind.

It was a triumph. At the end of the whole place erupted. My new human, like me, a true music-lover, threw his expensive hat high in the air. We shall stay together. He is a foreign correspondent with an illustrated journal in London and travels the planet covering the major news stories, an excellent way to keep you informed.

For a member of the kin to be a journalist is depressing. Inevitably our subject matter is war and its violent excesses.

In New York on the way to cover the Spanish-American War of ninety-eight, I revisited the Music Hall, now called Carnegie Hall, a much needed respite.

Since then I have been in Asia covering the Boxer Rebellion and the horrors of Peking. Now I am back in South Africa. The Boer business is very nasty. My artist sends back wonderfully executed drawings of Britishers falling heroically in battle. Reality is grimmer. The appalling effect of the new dum-dum bullets on human flesh is not suitable for home consumption.

Being a correspondent has become unbearable. I beg you to recall me. Trying to count the number of wars on Earth since Waterloo, I gave up on reaching twenty. The human race is totally irredeemable. Please allow me to return.

Everything has changed, I have discovered the Russians.

Tchaikovsky's music would sweep you off your feet. If you had feet. It calls up love, passion, drama and is fully of sweet melody.

Major orchestras are now sixty or more strong. Money and effort are lavished on the production of good music as well as upon war. Surely there is hope.

Human emotion seems to influence the composing of music, something as difficult to explain as music itself. Normally, I am attracted by the opposite sex but, occasionally, the same sex has the same effect. To communicate how strong these feelings can be is as impossible as explaining music to you.

Incidentally, mechanical vehicles have been developed which run on a dark oily substance pumped with great difficulty from beneath the surface of the earth, technology too limited to be significant.

President Woodrow Wilson is determined to maintain the splendid isolation of the United States. Americans will never join in this devastating European war. The overrunning of France by the Kaiser's army is imminent.

The White Russians will prevail.

Last night I heard Rachmaninov's Second Piano Concerto; a compelling opening followed by exciting, sweeping music which reaches dazzling crescendos. Then he wrings your heart with a romantic slow movement full of the sadness of lost love and aspiration.

Alcohol can only be enjoyed in illegal drinking dens called speakeasies where I've heard jazz, an exciting style of popular music. Prohibition is making Chicago a very dangerous place. I leave soon.

Mr Chamberlain has returned from Munich after a successful parley and has proclaimed "peace in our time". There will be no war.

The United States can never be persuaded to join in this European conflagration.

Despite the war I continue to hear good music, Beethoven's Seventh only yesterday. The second movement suited my mood admirably. That beautiful, inexorable melody ever repeating until it builds to a triumph. You believe the composer can find no sweeter variation, climb no further and yet he does and finally delivers you to his totally satisfying conclusion.

St Paul's Cathedral has survived within the roaring inferno of the City of London. On Earth beauty and devastation exist side by side and fill my being. Beethoven's sublime genius helps me survive.

I am back in Central Europe. The liberation should have been a happy time but stomach-churning is the only way to describe the aftermath of war. The destruction and deprivation are appalling. After the horrors of Dresden and Auschwitz I am willing to return to the kin.

Okay, so I'll stay. San Francisco is groovy. We live a life of, wow, ecstatic peace. Tolerance will infuse the planet so that all humankind can enjoy the pleasures of making love not war.

Why me? Hiroshima and Nagasaki; Dien Bien Phu and Kenya; Korea and Vietnam: endless conflict. As a war correspondent again, hunger and strife in Africa produces sights as unbearable as anything seen in the concentration camps.

There is nothing to be gained here but still you will not recall me.

I understand your concern about space programmes combined with the leap forward in weapon technology. My job in the news media gives access to many people with specialist knowledge who can find out more.

Regarding your other queries, the oil will run out in the next decade and, as a result of ecological mismanagement, unpolluted water will become a much scarcer commodity. However, most pundits do not envisage war, either nuclear or worse, over the dwindling resources and they are probably right.

The flight out to Nicaragua is booked for tomorrow.

The so-called Oil and Water Wars will come to nothing.

This world seems to have stepped backwards. Many have reverted to the old patterns of tribal loyalties. Empires are disintegrating into a kaleidoscope of warring factions desperate for diminishing resources. I hear and understand your demand that I return at once but I cannot.

My life is lived more intensely than ever before. Harrowing months in the various battle-zones are followed by ecstatic periods, on my return to Berlin, spent in the arms of Gerhard. He is the greatest love I have known. Just as you cannot understand music or the pleasures of alcohol, drugs and sex, so you can never comprehend love. It can override fear and logic. My love for Gerhard encompasses passion and physical pleasure approaching sublimation.

I shall not return. If I remain there is a possibility that you will not destroy Earth and all its people and in saving the world I should also be saving Gerhard.

Of course, my calculation may be incorrect. I have killed, though inadvertently, therefore you may well feel able to destroy me as well as these, too-dangerous humans. And, to tell true, my being is closer to humanity than the loveless spy who arrived so long ago.

I must take that chance. The whole of humanity may well destroy itself before long and solve your problem. Be assured that another agent sent to find me is doomed to fail and will simply constitute another life put at risk.

The saneness and sensibility of the kin are wonderful but that form of life is no longer possible for me.

I will never return.

The seriousness of your final order was fully comprehended. To remain now means I remain forever. So be it.

Here, the whole gamut of emotions is in my repertoire. After the temporary terrors of war comes the return to a civilised life; hot baths, good food, alcohol, a soft bed, sex and, of course, music.

Yes, there are still space programmes and if you feel that you must prevent humankind from spreading its unacceptable ways beyond its own world, I perfectly understand. If, as a result, disintegration by the kin threatens me as much as human war, those risks must be braved. No other choice lies open. Gerhard cannot travel with me therefore nothing can change my mind.

Grasping the idea of morality has been difficult. If humans can accept the concept of certain death then why not me? I have come to terms with disintegration whether from the kin or the many dangers of the planet.

Until the end comes, I shall wallow in the warmth of Gerhard's love. Before oblivion we shall enjoy, at the flip of a switch, the very best renderings of Mozart and Mendelssohn, Bach and Beethoven, Tchaikovsky, Rachmaninov and, of course, Haydn. Perhaps I have not been the perfect agent. My predictions have often proved wrong. Yet I did tell you, over two hundred years ago, that Joseph Haydn's music would live on long years after his death. And I was right.

This is my last communication. Just like humanity, I have become cynical, dissolute and not worth saving. However, I don't suppose it will come to...

About the Author

Lannah Battley, a Londoner by birth, now lives in West Wales. Among other things, she has been an actress and stage manager, a research laboratory assistant, a librarian and an administrator in a psychiatric hospital. Educated at the Godolphin and Latymer School, Hammersmith, she holds a BA Honours degree from the Open University.

Her novel *Either End of the Tunnel* was published last year. The first sequel is due in 2017.

Website: www.lannahbattley.co.uk

Also by Lannah Battley:

Either End of the Tunnel

A novel of parallel worlds in Victorian times.

"A rollercoaster of a book combining the genres of science fiction, historical fiction and thriller."

Diane Staphnill

"Pacy, densely plotted story of parallel worlds where the leading characters… battle against greed, abduction and murder."

Maria Goodess

55602916R00133

Made in the USA
Charleston, SC
29 April 2016